Published by Amanda McIntyre

ALL I WANT FOR CHRISTMAS
Copyright © 2016 by Amanda McIntyre

www.amandamcintyresbooks.com

Printed in the USA.

Cover design by Syneca Featherstone/Original Syn Graphics

Edited by Kristina Cook

Interior format ©

AMANDA MCINTYRE

ALL I WANT FOR CHRISTMAS

A Kinnison Legacy Holiday Novella

Chapter One

LIBERTY GLANCED AT THE SWEET, gooey cinnamon bun Betty had placed before her. There was a day when she could've downed two in rapid succession without so much as a flinch. Today, however, was different. She checked her cell phone for the hundredth time, seeing that she still had a good twenty minutes to wait.

"Would you like another warm-up of your coffee, hon?" Betty asked. The woman looked down at her, with concern in her soft brown eyes. She was the quintessential "mother" to many in the little town--certainly had been to Liberty since her controversial arrival a couple of years before.

"Maybe I should have a to-go box, Betty. I'm not sure I'm ready for this." She chewed on the corner of her lip, studying the picture Ellie Harrison at the shelter for women and children in Billings had given her. Ellie, a social worker, had moved to Billings from Chicago about a year ago and now ran the safe house for victims of abuse and violence toward women and children. She'd asked if she and Rein might be interested in being temporary foster parents to a child whose mother had been placed in jail awaiting sentencing for possession of drugs. Though they were often at the safe house helping out and had met the child in question on more than one occasion, having him twenty-four-seven was bound to be different.

Betty took a quick assessment of the late afternoon crowd in the café, then slid into the booth across from Liberty.

"You and Rein are perfect for this. It may not be something you'd wish to do forever, but it might provide you both with a bit of a pleasant distraction from…you know."

Liberty placed her phone on the table. Betty was, of course, referring to the fact that she and her husband had been in the throes of trying to conceive after miscarrying. "You know, maybe I have to accept that I'm not supposed to have children, Betty." The thought twisted her heart. Ever since she'd discovered she had two stepbrothers—Wyatt and Dalton Kinnison—her life had completely changed. Seeing the love and warmth they'd created at the Last Hope Ranch, meeting the folks in End of the Line, and falling in love with Rein Mackenzie had given her hope of one day having a large, noisy family of her own.

Betty took her hand and patted it. "I've never known a woman more deserving of being a mother than you, honey. Sometimes these things take time. Meanwhile, being a foster parent allows you to share all that love with a child who desperately needs it."

She pushed away the fear that she and Rein might never have children of their own. "I understand that logically, Betty. And part of me is more than ready to step up and do that. But the other part is afraid that doing so will serve as a painful reminder to Rein of what we don't have."

"Aw, hon, Rein isn't that like that. He'd lasso the moon for you if you asked him for it--you know that."

Liberty nodded.

"And the man is for certain determined to have a family. He was an only child before the accident and when Jed took him in, raising him alongside Wyatt and Dalton, he came to realize how important having family really is."

Betty's affirmation of what Liberty already knew to be true made her smile. Currently, her husband had been busy along with Clay, Dalton, and Tyler in the process of renovating and updating the old building next door to launch Betty's new addition, the Sunrise Bakery, in time for its grand Christmas opening. And while there were days when he was so exhausted he simply fell into bed, she had to credit him with somehow finding the drive to make her feel wanted each and every day—sometimes twice a day.

Betty stood. "Speak of the devil."

Rein walked through the café door, sending its newly added sleigh bells to jingle merrily. "Hey, Betty," he said as he removed his Stetson and gloves. "Can I get a cup of coffee, please?"

"Comin' right up, darlin'," she said as she skirted through the maze of tables.

Liberty turned her face up to accept Rein's kiss, his lips chilled from working in the hollowed-out building next door. They had hoped to have everything enclosed by Thanksgiving, but they'd run into multiple code issues as they took down walls and set to repositioning water and electrical lines.

"How's it going over there?" she asked. Liberty had been waiting patiently, reconfiguring her plans with Betty each time a new problem arose.

Her husband's clear blue eyes captured hers, as they had on a daily basis since the first day they met at the bus station in Billings. She'd looked far different back then, her brittle persona still raw from the bad blood she'd left behind and wary of the new family she was about to walk into. How quickly life can change in a couple of years, she thought.

"Getting there. Tyler's rerouting the plumbing and that's forcing a delay in Julie and the boys moving into the apartment upstairs." He sighed and gave Betty a grateful smile as she placed a steaming white mug in front of him. "Sorry, Betty. I'd really hoped to have you up and running by Christmas. It may take a miracle to accomplish that with all the delivery delays we've had."

Betty patted his shoulder. "Honey, I've seen what a little faith can do. If I've learned nothing else running a café seven days a week, it's that patience often reaps its own rewards." She offered Liberty a wink before scooting away to serve another customer.

"What was that all about?" Rein asked with a curious expression. He blew across the top of his coffee to cool it down.

"Support. I maybe got a tad panicky earlier…about all this." Liberty looked out the window, pressing her lips together to prevent her concerns from spilling out again. It was a frosty late November evening. The scent of snow was in the air, though no weather station had mentioned it in the forecast. Then again, End of the Line quite often fell between the meteorological cracks, being up in the mountains. Despite the overcast skies, she'd seen a great white owl while climbing into her car that morning. Without thinking, she'd waved a friendly greeting to the stately looking bird. "Hello, Jed," she'd called out. The owl's large gold eyes blinked twice before he'd spread his wings and soared from the tree near their front porch to the roof of Rein's woodshed barn. The owl, spotted by members of the Kinnison clan and the local community, was no longer considered a mystery but now a legend. It was a common belief among both Kinnsion family members and close friends that the owl possessed the spirit of Jed Kinnison, stepfather of Wyatt and Dalton, as well as to Rein Mackenzie, his nephew. The three had been thrown together under Jed's care after tragedy struck each of their young lives. Those boys, now men with families of their own, were making sure Jed's legacy lived on in the historical, once-mining town.

"Are you having second thoughts?"

Rein's voice jarred Liberty from her thoughts. He reached

for her hand. "Sweetheart, we don't have to do this. Not if it's going to be too hard on you."

The bells over the door jingled again, pulling her attention to the familiar woman who'd just entered, a little boy, barely over four, clinging to her hand. Ellie felt that meeting publicly might be best. It would give the boy a chance to warm up to Rein and Liberty before they took him home.

Her heart squeezed at the sight of his small face, framed in a bright red knit stocking cap. His cheeks were flushed from the cold, his blue eyes filled with caution. Liberty watched him scan the patrons, an adult wariness replacing the joy that one would normally see in a child this age. There was no sparkle, no childlike wonder. Only an apparent vacancy. She grabbed Rein's hand as they both stood to greet Miss Ellie.

"Hello," Ellie said, her gaze sweeping from Liberty to Rein and then to the table. "Have you already ordered? Maybe we could sit down and join you." Without waiting for a reply, she bent down to help the child from his outer coverings and ushered him into the booth before removing her own coat and scooting in beside him.

Rein nudged her and Liberty slid into the booth across from their dining companions, making room for Rein to sit beside her.

"This is Cody Ross." The kind woman placed her arm around his tiny shoulders. "Cody, you remember Mr. and Mrs. Mackenzie from the house?"

The young boy ducked beneath Ellie's arm, shielding his face in her shoulder.

She smiled and hugged the boy. "It's okay, Cody. They are some of my best friends and I know they'd like to be yours, too. Why, I bet if you wanted, Mr. Mackenzie might even take you to see his horses at the Last Hope Ranch."

The boy peeked at Rein.

"It's true,". Rein said with a nod. "We have a lot of horses and one of our dogs just had a litter of puppies. Do you like puppies?"

The boy glanced at Liberty, then back to Rein and nodded. He cautiously extracted himself from Ellie's embrace.

Liberty's eyes stung from unshed tears. She wanted nothing more than to scoop up the little boy and hug him. Her fear of whether she could love a child not her own was immediately replaced with that of whether she'd be able to let go of this one when the time came. "Do you like Christmas trees, Cody?" Liberty asked. "We've been waiting to put ours up." She didn't add that the reason had been her melancholy about the holidays in general. Liberty hadn't been able to muster much Christmas spirit, despite being very happy for friends and family in the throes of having children—starting their families.

"I never had one," he said softly. He rubbed his small fist down his cheek and glanced at Ellie, seemingly unsure if that was the appropriate answer.

Liberty smiled encouragingly. "Then this will be a very special tree indeed. One that you can pick out. How about that?"

His eyes narrowed briefly, followed by a barely noticeable nod before his gaze fell on the giant gooey cinnamon roll that Liberty had ordered.

"Would you like to try a bite? Betty makes the best cinnamon rolls on the planet."

"It's true," Betty said with a grin for the boy. "At least, that's what they tell me." She placed a cup of coffee on the table for Ellie. In front of Cody she put a small mug of hot cocoa. "You looked like a marshmallow kind of guy. Here," she said, "you'll probably need a spoon."

Cody accepted the spoon, then tentatively reached for the pastry.

"Oh, here. Let me help you with that." Liberty sliced off a piece and placed it on the small plate Betty had brought.

Cody picked up the bite with tiny fingers and took a nibble.

Liberty held her breath, awaiting the little boy's reaction.

"Do you like that?" Ellie asked, finally cutting the tension.

He thought for a moment, then smiled and nodded.

Rein leaned back with a grin as Cody quickly devoured the rest and reached for more.

"How about we get some bacon to go with that? Then maybe Mrs. Mackenzie will share a bit more with you," Ellie offered. "Would you like that?"

The little boy nodded. For the next thirty minutes Liberty watched entranced by how the young boy's demeanor changed from sullen to seemingly content. She wondered what kind of things those soulful little eyes had seen. Images of her childhood drifted into her thoughts, remembering things that no child should have to experience.

Ellie caught her gaze and smiled as though understanding the sum of Liberty's thoughts. She turned to the boy. "Cody, how would you like to go with Mr. and Mrs. Mackenzie to see their house, and stay for a short visit? Maybe you could help with the new puppies?"

"They're only a few weeks old and you'd have to be very gentle. Could you do that?" Liberty took his tiny hand in hers. The mere touch produced a strange lump in her throat.

Cody drew his hand away and, pushing to his knees, whispered in Ellie's ear.

She smiled and glanced at Rein and Liberty. "Mr. Mackenzie isn't your father, no, but he and Mrs. Mackenzie have offered to let you stay with them for a while. But I'll be up to visit you in a day or two."

"We've got a special room ready for you, buddy," Rein said. "You'll have your own bed. Your own toys."

"Tractors?"

Rein blinked, then grinned. "Sure, absolutely. John Deere. And when the weather clears we'll go down to my brother's ranch and see the horses."

"I like horses," Cody piped up without reservation.

"Then we'll need to get you a pair of real cowboy boots, I'm thinking. What do you say?"

"And a hat… like yours?" He pointed to Rein's perched on the hook by the booth.

Liberty caught Rein's eye and grinned. The little guy wasn't the least bit shy once he felt comfortable.

"Well, then, Cody, I guess let's go get your things out of the car," Ellie said.

Rein stood. "I'll go take care of the bill. Liberty can go with you. I'll be right out."

Ellie handed the boy's coat to her. "Into the deep end, girlfriend."

That's what I'm afraid of. She knelt in front of the little boy. A million questions and concerns spun in her brain. Only one kept swirling to the forefront. Can I do this? She glanced up at Ellie as she stood.

Ellie smiled. "It's going to be fine."

Liberty looked down at the little boy who stood holding his mitten-clad hand out to take hers and her heart took a tumble. "Come on, let's go get your things."

Rein sifted through the bills in his wallet as Betty waited. "She looks like a natural."

Rein glanced over his shoulder and saw that Liberty had picked up Cody and held him in one arm as she accepted his little backpack from Ellie. He'd never seen anything quite as beautiful as the woman he loved holding a child.

As much as he knew they'd care for Cody, he couldn't help but wish for a child of his own. "Thanks, Betty. We're both a little nervous, I guess."

She waved away his concern. "You two will be the best thing that little tyke needs right now. Your Uncle Jed would be so proud."

Rein stepped out into the wintry dusk. Snow had begun to fall by the time they'd said their goodbyes to Ellie and pulled into the home that he and Liberty had designed. It had been built in record time with the help of the entire community. After Rein's and Liberty's tumultuous beginnings—including a sizzling summer affair, a fire that partially destroyed the old main Kinnison home, Liberty having to testify against her gangster ex-boss in Vegas, and Rein's gunshot wounds--they'd married the day the trial had ended.

By then, Rein's brother Wyatt had already started construction on their home located on the Kinnsion property. It was a short drive to the ranch, where Aimee and Wyatt now lived with their daughter, Grace. Dalton, the next oldest in line, and his wife, Angelique, also lived on another area of the extensive Kinnison land, closer to the mountains they so dearly loved. A true native to the area, Angelique's Crow culture flowed through every facet of her and Dalton's life with their daughter, almost nine, and a new baby boy, Sawyer, born this past June. The three men were raised together solely by Montana rancher Jed Kinnison after tragedy had struck each of their lives when they were teens. Wyatt and Dalton had been adopted after their mother abandoned them, and Rein had come to live at his uncle's ranch after his parents had been killed in a car accident— his mother had been Jed's only sister. Together, Rein, Wyatt, and Dalton had created a strong, unbreakable bond that had thus far weathered a multitude of storms. With families of their own now, they furthered that bond with the tradition of rotating Sunday family dinners at each other's houses.

Rein turned off the ignition and glanced back at the boy strapped into the new car seat. They had researched dozens before deciding on this one—one they felt was safest for his size. A strange yet familiar tug pulled on his heart. Was this how Jed must have felt when he looked at the three misfit teenage boys fate had bestowed on him?

Liberty followed his gaze. "Are you okay?" she asked. "You haven't said much on the way home." Together they paused, watching the slumbering child. Outside the snow fell in soft, giant flakes. "We should probably get him inside. I don't think freezing him is wise." Liberty patted his shoulder.

He grabbed her hand and leaned over to kiss her. "I love you."

She cupped his cheek. "Hold that thought. You get Cody, I'll get his bag."

Rein loved how effortlessly they seemed to work together as a team to get the sleepy child ready for bed.

Liberty plugged in the small lamp with a muted light so if he woke, he wouldn't be afraid of the dark. On the nightstand were two framed pictures—one of him and his mom in better days, and a smaller one of Rein and Liberty with their dogs.

Liberty bent down and brushed a wisp of hair from the child's forehead before placing a kiss there. She then joined Rein, who stood at the door waiting for her. "Do you think I need to sleep in here tonight?" she asked him.

A low, mournful hoot—that of an owl—sounded from outside the window.

Rein chuckled. "Jed's keeping watch." He rubbed her shoulders. "Come on, I'm still hanging onto that thought like you asked."

A few moments later, he lay in bed and watched Liberty go through her nightly routine—she washed her face, brushed her teeth, would start to climb into bed, have an afterthought and go back to check the bedroom window to be sure it was locked—everything she'd done nightly since they'd married. Tonight, he couldn't put his finger on the odd emotions playing inside him as he watched her checking the locks. "Darlin', you know that Antonio and his men will be locked away for a very long time, and I won't let anything happen to you."

She folded her arms, tossed him a glance, and looked back at the snowy night.

"What is it, sweetheart?" He climbed out of bed, walked up behind her and pulled her close, wrapping his arms around her.

"It feels right...having him here." She leaned against him, holding his arms to her. "Is that weird?"

He gave her a quick squeeze. "If it is, then I must be weird, too. I think he fits right in."

"What if he wakes up and gets scared?"

He kissed the top of her head. "We'll hear him. That monitor you bought has both sound and visual. Now, come to bed," he whispered as he nuzzled the sweet, warm curve of her neck.

"Maybe we should shut the door."

Rein thought a moment, shrugged, and complied with his wife's wish. He agreed that he wasn't yet ready for that talk. He was halfway back to the bed, where Liberty had dropped her robe and lay in her next-to-nothing gown. He'd been thinking for the better part of two hours of how he'd peel it off her.

"Wait." She pointed to the door. "Maybe open it a little...so we can hear."

Rein eyed her, finding this new side of his wife—usually uninhibited when it came to their lovemaking—quite interesting.

With a sigh and a definite semi, Rein returned to the door. "He seemed pretty zonked to me, sweetheart, but if it makes you feel more at ease…." The matter of how wide to leave the door open was the strangest foreplay Rein had ever experienced. "How about there?" He'd positioned it according to her instructions for at least the third time. He looked back at Liberty who now lay on her side. She had a wicked smile. It dawned on him then that she'd been playing him with the dexterity of a maestro.

He narrowed his gaze, hooked his thumbs in his boxer briefs and stripped, pleased when her eyes widened at his already firm erection. He crawled over the bed, and she accepted him with a kiss unlike any they'd ever shared. He was about to take things to the next level when Liberty's hand came between their lips.

"Sssh, did you hear something?" Her eyes searched the ceiling as she lay beneath him.

"Probably the wind," he spoke through her lovely fingers. His mouth barred from her face, he chose to focus on another set of his wife's best features. He felt her body relax, succumbing to his touch, pressing her hips to his. He revisited her mouth, never tiring of the sounds she made in her throat when he gave her pleasure.

"Baby," she whispered in his ear.

He braced on his elbows. "I didn't hear anything."

Liberty chuckled as she drew back the covers. "That was meant for you," she purred, trailing her finger down his chest.

Wasting no time, he found his way under the covers. The freedom of not having to concern themselves with protection was some of the best sex he'd had with Liberty—and after their whirlwind, erotically-charged summer affair, that said a lot.

He lifted her hips to meet him, her sighs tripping his heart as he entered slowly, pausing to relish the sheer connection they shared.

"Do you think we should shut off the light? Just in case?" she whispered, her hips already moving in languid rhythm to his.

Rein had already begun the descent into sexual bliss. "No time," he said, groaning softly as he plunged deep, and began the syncopated dance as old as time. "You feel amazing, sweetheart." Rein's body was tight with need. Part of him delighted in his fantasy of seeing her belly swollen with his child. The idea made him horny as hell and that fever produced an adrenaline-driven passion that nearly consumed him at times.

Her fingers clawed the flesh of his ass. Her face upturned, holding his gaze, as though willing conception to happen. Daring the universe not to ignore this pure love between them.

Her mouth dropped open with what was usually followed by a loud and seductive mention of his name as she reached her climax. He pressed a finger to her lips and smiled, replacing it with a fierce kiss that toppled both of them over the edge in a duet of soft groans and muted sighs.

"I'm thirsty."

Rein rolled to his side, making certain they were covered. "Uh, okay, buddy. We'll get you some water. How will that be?"

The small boy stood in the open doorway, his tiny fist rubbing at his eyes. Rein realized his boxer briefs lay on the floor where he'd shimmied out of them. He shot a look at Liberty for assistance.

"Just a sec, I'll help you," Liberty said.

She tugged her gown around her hips and he realized

how intense their lovemaking had been. She reached for her robe draped at the end of the bed.

Rein made a mental note to stick a pair of fresh skivvies under the mattress for just such emergencies.

Crisis averted. The young child didn't seem to be shocked or traumatized.

Unlike Rein.

He released a sigh, checked the door to make sure the two had gone before scrambling out of bed and wiggling back into his underwear. He dove under the covers just as the pair returned. Liberty carried a small glass of water and a book.

"Okay, get up in there." She put the glass on the nightstand.

Rein watched, unsure how he felt about this. After all, this wasn't his kid. Cody giggled as the mattress bounced and he crawled to Liberty's pillow and lay down.

"Uh…" he managed to get out before the little boy turned to him with a wide grin.

"Wrestling is fun. I've seen it on T.V.," Cody said.

Rein caught Liberty's smile.

"Just one story," she remarked. "Then it's back to bed."

"Can we wrestle?"

"No," he and Liberty replied in unison.

"What we mean is, you are too young—" She looked to him for support.

"And we have a very busy day tomorrow. You'll need your sleep if you want to see the horses."

Liberty puffed up her pillows and sat on the bed, crossing her ankles. She drew Cody under her arm.

"What is this story?"

"Well, it's about a little boy. Only he's a baby. It's called *A Cowboy's Christmas*, and it's one of Mr. Mackenzie's favorite books from when he was little."

Cody looked over Liberty's arm at Rein, his expression indicating he couldn't envision Rein ever being small.

Rein turned on his side, tucking his arm under his head as he listened to his wife read the timeless story that Jed used to read every Christmas at the holiday parties he gave at the Kinnison ranch. Though he'd been older than Cody, he cherished those times, tucking them deep inside. Many years had gone by after Jed's death when the tattered book sat on a shelf in his uncle's library. Fortunately, the book was spared any damage from the arsonist's fire that nearly claimed Liberty as well as Wyatt's then-pregnant wife, Aimee. It had been Liberty's quick thinking, her fierce loyalty to her newly found stepbrothers—Wyatt and Dalton—that had given her the courage to go back to Vegas and testify against her former boss at a club where she'd once danced. At first, Rein hadn't trusted her. She was different than any woman he'd known. She'd worn her dark hair streaked with neon blue and coated her eyes in heavy makeup. Her goth look was only exceeded by her snarly, independent attitude which he would come to understand after hearing about her childhood.

Their courtship—as it were—had been rocky, akin to a made for TV movie or perhaps a juicy novel. But all had turned out well and now, after two years of married bliss, both were ready—more than ready—to start their family. Having been an only child, he wanted a big, boisterous, chaotic family. He was pulled from his thoughts at the sound of Liberty's voice.

"What you do for the least of them, you do unto me." She paused. "The end."

Rein's lids drooped heavily. He started when he felt a tap on his shoulder.

"Can you carry him back to bed?" she mouthed.

Blinking a few times to awaken his brain, he gave her a

quick nod.

Pulling the boy from where he'd snuggled in next to his wife, Rein marveled how little he weighed. He tucked him in his arms, cradling him against his chest. Cody's little body felt so small, so vulnerable. How could someone, especially a mother, disregard such a precious gift?

The little boy yawned as Rein tucked the covers around him. He'd made the bed himself, slightly lower to the ground to accommodate short legs. He'd used a cattle brand to burn the Kinnison logo into the wooden bed frame.

Cody turned on his side and snuggled into his pillow.

Rein started to leave.

"Is it okay if I call you daddy… just while I'm here?"

The voice with its whisper-soft request stopped Rein in his tracks. He glanced back, meeting the blue eyes looking up at him. Rein kneeled by the bed. His heart squeezed when the boy's tiny hand darted from beneath the blanket and touched his.

"Cody, you understand I'm not your father. But that doesn't mean I wouldn't be proud to be your dad."

The child seemed to ponder his words. "I'll only do it when I'm here. Miss Ellie likes it better when I call you Mr. and Mrs. Mackenzie."

Rein nodded. He didn't want to upset the protocol Ellie had implemented, but this was his home. "Tell you what- -around here, you can call us mom and dad, okay? Would that make you feel better?"

Cody nodded.

He ruffled the little boy's shaggy brown hair. "Okay, pard-ner, it's time to sleep. Horses don't take kindly to grumpy little boys."

Cody grinned.

Rein got to the door and looked back. "G'night, Cody."

"Night, Dad."

Tears stung the back of Rein's eyes and he nodded, swallowing the lump in his throat.

Chapter Two

LIBERTY AWOKE TO THE WELCOMING scent of coffee and pancakes. She lay a moment in the dusky light of morning and listened to the muted conversation wafting up the stairs from the kitchen. It'd been over a week since Cody had come into their lives with an ease that both delighted and terrified Liberty. An unbridled peal of giggling caused her to grin. Not wanting to be left out, she climbed from bed, slipped on her jeans, some cozy socks, and a roomy sweatshirt, and then headed downstairs. She paused at the kitchen door, listening to the conversation between Rein and Cody. Her heart squeezed as she entered and observed the sight before her.

Cody stood on a small stepstool, his little body wrapped in an apron with strings that wrapped three times around him. Rein, at his side in T-shirt and jeans, was carefully instructing him in the art of cooking pancakes. "You boys are up awfully early this morning." She was drawn to the coffee pot, helping herself to a steaming mug of motivation.

"Dad's showing me how to make pancakes."

Dad? The reference brought an unexpected flip to her heart, followed by a world of caution. They'd be wise to remember that this was a temporary situation. As much as she wanted to, it wasn't wise to give her heart so completely to this little boy. Eventually, he'd be leaving. It wouldn't be fair to any of them.

Rein glanced over his shoulder and caught her staring at them. As if on cue, Cody turned, mirroring Rein's questioning look.

It was startling to think how quickly it seemed they'd bonded. Already Cody had picked up on some of Rein's habits. Coupled with the fact they both had blue eyes and bright smiles, it was difficult to remember he wasn't theirs.

She cleared her throat, mentally scolding herself for imagining the similarities. "So, is breakfast almost ready?" She slid onto one of the stools at the end of the massive kitchen island Rein had designed. They'd both wanted the kitchen to be big enough for family gatherings.

Rein plucked Cody up under the arms and, to a squeal of delight, plopped him on a stool next to Liberty. With a light-hearted demeanor that she'd not seen in weeks, Rein served up three plates of pancakes with bacon on the side.

He put a short cup of milk in front of Cody and, bringing over the carafe, leaned down to give Liberty a kiss before refilling her cup.

"Good morning, beautiful," he said quietly, before kissing her again.

"It appears to be," she replied, searching his eyes.

"It is now." He sat on the other side of Cody and proceeded to cut up the child's pancakes. "I promised Cody we'd take him this week to see Santa. Heard something about him coming in on Thursday at the town square." He tossed Cody a grin as he slathered the boy's pancakes with syrup. "Only the real stuff around here, buddy."

The bond between them had been instant. Liberty wasn't sure how it was that her husband so readily compartmentalized his emotions when it came to the little boy. She loved seeing Rein having such fun with Cody, but she feared it was going to be difficult for him when it came time for Cody to leave. Perhaps for everyone. She wondered how other foster families managed the emotional risk. "What's on the agenda for the day, guys?" she asked, eying the two.

"I heard Hank is flying into Billings around noon. Clay is heading down with Julie to pick him up."

"What about the boys?" Liberty asked. The new manager of Betty's upcoming bakery enterprise, Julie had recently moved to End of the Line after a dangerously abusive marriage. Now single, it appeared that her newly rekindled relationship with Hank Richardson was getting serious.

"Sally's got them today. She needs some help going through a couple of closets. She seems to be on a cleaning spree. Chris and Kyle are her manpower."

Liberty gasped and checked the clock. "Oh, my gosh, I forgot that I'm supposed to meet with her today. She wanted to ask my thoughts on color schemes and décor for the nursery."

Rein's attention was focused on Cody. It was as though the little guy had never before eaten pancakes. "Whoa, slow down, buddy. There's more if you want them."

Liberty waited a beat. "So I guess you're taking the day off, then?"

"Huh?" Rein looked up at that. "I can't. I promised Betty we'd try to get the bakery up and running for her holiday opening." He glanced at Cody, then back to Liberty. "What's your afternoon like?" he asked, seemingly aware suddenly that they now had a third person to consider in their daily lives. "I'll take Cody in with me this morning and he can help me do some measuring. We could meet at the diner for lunch."

Liberty saw where he was headed. "That could work. The planning committee is meeting after lunch at the diner to plan the Christmas Walk. He could come with me."

Cody wrinkled his nose.

"I'm pretty sure there might be a candy cane in that

for you somewhere, buddy." Rein patted the young boy's shoulder.

They cleaned the kitchen and Liberty helped Cody dress in the only other outfit that was in his backpack—one she happened to recognize as back-to-school clothing they'd bought and donated for kids who lived at the shelter. Tucking him into his coat and mittens, she waved at the two as Rein buckled Cody into the car. He moved a few tools over from his truck. "See you at noon," he called with a wave.

She watched from the door as they took off down the lane. She was learning quickly how one child could so quickly change your life. And Sally was about to take on two. With a sigh, she closed the door with her sights on a warm shower.

Later that day, she sat at her committee meeting for the Christmas Walk, helping to make final preparations for one of the most beloved of all events in End of the Line. Seated in the private party room at the diner was Aimee Kinnison, committee chairwoman; Rosie Waters from Rosie's Antiques; Nan, the owner of Nan's Sporting Goods; Betty from the café; and Liberty. Sally, very pregnant now with twins, had bowed out of the event planning this year, and Angelique was at home today with Sawyer, who was in the midst of teething.

"He's adorable," Aimee said as she looked lovingly at the little boy resting between two chairs they'd pushed together. He was fast asleep, and Liberty had put his coat over him. In truth, Cody looked like an angel with his soft brown hair curling around his face.

They'd chosen the café for its central location, and traditionally the room was quiet. Today, however, their meeting was challenged with the cacophony of drills and hammering from the renovation of the building next door.

"You know," Rosie said above the din, "we could meet next time at the store. I should have thought of that sooner."

Betty, who'd only just found a moment to join the group after the lunch crowd cleanup, shook her head. "I appreciate you all meeting here. I don't like to leave Jerry alone after his stroke. I know it was mild and he's really doing much better, but that day was... well, horrible, and I guess I like to stick close."

"Oh, absolutely, honey," Rosie said. "I understand." She patted Betty's arm.

Betty set a plate of fresh cookies in the middle of the table. "Besides, I need you all to taste these. It's a recipe I found from Bernice, an old neighbor back in Iowa, before we moved out here. They're called Snickerdoodles—kind of a cross between shortbread and a sugar cookie with a cinnamon sprinkle. They remind me of the holidays." She glanced at her watch. "Oh, and...wait for it." She held up her finger, garnering everyone's attention, and the noise on the other side of the wall stopped almost as though on cue. "They always take a break at one-thirty." She sighed. "Now we have approximately twenty-five minutes to go over things. I figure it keeps us on task, right?" She looked at the ladies.

Aimee grinned and nodded. "Now let's see...."

At that moment, Cody, who'd been blissfully sleeping through the noise, awoke. He sat up, rubbed his eyes, and scanned the circle of women before looking up at Liberty. "Can we go home now?"

She looked down at his sleepy little, cherub-like face. It had been an extraordinary day for the little guy. Trudging off with Rein before eight a.m., then spending time with Betty's husband Jerry, sitting on a stool and coloring while Rein prepped his workers for the day.

Liberty caught Aimee's eye at Cody's reference to going

home. Aimee had thought she was pregnant a few months back, but the test turned out to be a false positive. She and Wyatt definitely wanted another child, and if Aimee had her way, she'd get a boy to carry on the Kinnison name.

"In a bit, Cody, we just need to discuss a few things, okay?"

"I have to go potty."

Liberty met the gazes of the women around her. Thus far, this had been Rein's job.

"Bathroom is 'round back through the kitchen. The public restrooms are being expanded." Betty stood to let Liberty and Cody by. "You need Jerry to help?"

Liberty guided Cody past the chairs and took his hand. "We're good, thanks," she said with more bravado than she truly felt. This was brand new territory and while she knew she could probably call on Rein to help, she wanted to... well, to be a mom.

They arrived outside the cubicle of a bathroom and had to wait for one of the construction workers to finish using the facility. Cody danced, holding his miniscule crotch. At one point, Liberty had considered how private the alley outside the back door might be.

Once the room was vacated, she flipped on the light and observed the one stool--far too tall for him to reach alone. She figured her options were to have him sit, or hold him up so he could do his business.

Together they stared at the toilet.

"Miss Ellie has a step-stool."

Fine. That settled that question. He did know how to pee standing up--this was good. Liberty knelt and undid his little jeans, her fingers feeling clumsy and awkward. Finally, she was able to jostle his jeans down over his training pants—a

marvelous gift that Ellie had tucked in his backpack, and something they would soon need to restock. "Yeah, well,

I'm going to have to be your step-stool today." She flipped open the lid and turned him toward the toilet. "Just hang on, buddy. I'm going to lift you up… like this." She grabbed him beneath the arms, planting her feet firmly for balance. Liberty waited, trying to be considerate to the fact that he might not be as comfortable with her as with his mother, or with Ellie or even Rein. "Okay, you can go ahead… anytime, Cody. Just aim and you know… fire away."

His little legs dangled above the stool, his jeans circled like a dead weight around the real cowboy boots Rein had bought him—heavy little cowboy boots, at that.

"I don't think I can. I'm too high."

"Fair enough." Liberty lowered the boy to a height that wasn't quite so high as when Simba lifted his son to the herd in The Lion King. "Better?"

"I want the stool."

"Yeah, me too," she said, her shoulders beginning to cramp. "But right now, we don't have much choice." It dawned on her that maybe he'd be okay with sitting, which sounded good in theory, but could open up another set of challenges. "Do you want to sit, instead?" She began to lower him.

"No!" he screamed, wiggling his little body to make his point.

She nearly lost her grip, which was where her mental state was quickly headed. "Okay, okay." Sure of how to handle most things in her life—good God, she'd survived a fire, and a paid assassin—her brain scrambled to find a solution. "Listen, Cody. You do know how to pee like a big boy, right?"

He nodded. "Dad… Mr. Mackenzie showed me."

"Yay, that's great." So the child wasn't exactly an old hand at this. "Okay, then, all you have to do is… like what Mr. Mackenzie showed you."

"He had a step-stool, too."

There was a step-stool in the bathroom? Where had that come from? "Okay, then. So, let's pretend you have the step-stool."

"He said I could call him dad."

The muscles in her arms burned. Her days of daily exercise as an exotic dancer in Vegas seemed like a million years ago. "Can you please just try to go, Cody?" She tried not to sound too desperate.

"I'll try." He bent his head as though lining up his target.

There was a knock on the door before it opened and Rein stepped in. "Betty said you guys might need--"

Startled, Liberty turned to look at him, too late to realize that Cody—ready to fire--was poised as a human water pistol. A steady stream arched with fair distance for a four-year-old across the tiny bathroom, leaving a trail across Rein's work boots.

Rein followed both her and Cody's stupefied gazes to where a dark line appeared with near precision across the toes of his chamois-colored boots.

"I did it!" Cody held his arms high in victory. Liberty, nearly losing her grasp, had to grab him around the middle.

She needed a drink.

"I peed like you showed me." Cody's voice was laced with utter glee.

Liberty, glad the ordeal was over, repositioned the boy's pants and lifted him to the sink to wash his hands.

Rein had taken a wad of paper towels to clean up the tiny trail Cody had left behind.

"Sorry, guess I'm new to this part," Liberty said to Rein's reflection in the mirror.

He grinned and kissed the top of her head, then Cody's. "We'll do a little target practice at home, okay, buddy? My mom used to float Cheerios in the toilet so we could practice."

Liberty caught his sexy grin.

"You girls didn't know what you were missing."

The three exited the bathroom together, Cody more than pleased with himself. Rein, at ease, kissed her on the temple and went on his merry way, and she felt as though she'd been spun through a rinse cycle. By the time they rejoined the planning meeting, they were nearly through the agenda.

Aimee, the consummate teacher, scanned her list. "Okay, now is Re--" she stopped suddenly, realizing her near faux pas. "Reindeers… I mean is Santa" --she emphasized the name-- "planning to bring his reindeer to the park this year?"

Liberty cleared her throat to hide her smile. "We did hear that he plans to be here. Not sure yet on the reindeer, or if he'll be borrowing horses instead for the parade. You know how nervous reindeer can be around crowds."

Cody, nursing a cookie that Betty had given him, looked in wide-eyed wonder at the women as though amazed that they seemed to know the jolly old guy on a personal level.

Betty judiciously changed the topic. "And hopefully we'll have the bakery up and running to the point where we can serve my special holiday cupcakes to parade goers this year." The End of the Line lighted holiday parade had in recent years drawn folks not only from the surrounding smaller towns, but also folks from the city looking for that small-town holiday experience.

"I like cupcakes." Cody smiled at Betty.

She gave him a quick hug. "A boy after my own heart. It's been way too long since this town had a proper bakery."

"Agreed," Nan said as she smacked her palm to the table. "Those bear claws they have at the Git and Go are the most pathetic excuse for a Godda--"

"Nan," Betty warned with a tip of her head toward Cody.

"Gosh darn pastry," Nan finished instead. "We need to be able to buy fresh products without all those chemicals and preservatives in 'em."

Nan, who'd started the local sporting goods store with her taxidermist husband the better part of thirty years ago, now ran the uniquely decorated store alone. She was a hard woman, self-sufficient. Few filters. Not used to kids. Never had them. Never wanted them. Still, it fascinated Liberty that Nan was the greatest advocate of the holiday events in End of the Line. It had been rumored that, at one time in Jed Kinnison's later years, he and Nan had dated a few times. But to this day, it remained pure speculation.

"You'll take care of the holiday wreaths on the utility poles again, Nan?" Aimee asked, checking her three-ring, color-coded binder.

"Will do. And I'll have Tyler check the lights along the top of the store fronts. Those…darn things look so pretty at night. Great idea Jed Kinnison had." She nodded. The lights outlined the tops of each building surrounding the square and stayed up year-round, so that only minor repairs and replacements needed to be done on them.

"What about the tree in the town square?" Rosie asked. "Will we have one this year? I miss that tradition of the lights on the stores and the tree all being lit at once."

"Oh," Aimee finished, chewing a bit of cookie. "Wyatt said he and the guys would take care of it."

Betty's eyebrows rose. There hadn't been a tree in the square for years…not since Jed Kinnison left this earth. "I don't know how you managed that, honey. But kudos to you." She raised her water glass to Aimee.

"It wasn't me." Aimee held her hands up. "It was Grace. She seems to have a thing for Christmas trees this year. Every time she sees one on the television or in a store her little eyes light up. When I mentioned something about the tree to Wyatt over dinner, Gracie clapped her hands and tried to say 'Christmas tree.' Adorable, but slaughtered the words. Nonetheless, that was all it took. Wyatt said his baby girl was going to have the biggest, best Christmas tree in the state." She looked at the others. "And… I'm not sure anyone is going to believe it, but he wants to have a holiday open house out at the ranch this year. Just like Jed used to do."

Betty shook her head with a low chuckle. "That little girl has her daddy wrapped around her little finger already."

Aimee smiled. "Yeah, I saw that coming the day the doctor laid her in his arms."

Liberty felt a tug on her sweater and realized the meeting had dragged on longer than she'd expected. "Okay, email me a list of the stores participating in the Christmas window decorating contest. I've got a little guy here who needs his afternoon nap."

Cody waved at the ladies as they left. He was nodding off as they pulled up to the house. Carrying him inside, she let her purse fall just inside the door and carried him upstairs to his room and lay down on his little bed, drawing him close as they both drifted to sleep.

The following Tuesday, Rein eyeballed the space as he and Clay positioned one of the cabinets that would become the bakery's prep area. With Liberty's design help, he'd taken out the wall separating the two kitchen areas, providing a better utilization of storage and refrigeration for both businesses. That, however, wasn't what was on his mind. It'd made him uneasy to leave Liberty alone at home to deal with Ellie coming to pick up Cody—she was taking him to visit his mom for a few hours. The woman had a right to see her son, of course, and he knew very little about her, but didn't Cody have the right to a normal childhood and a safe and happy home? Had his mom provided that when she made the choices that landed her in the pickle she now found herself in?

"It's starting to come together. You, on the other hand, look like you're hanging by a thread." Clay Saunders, Rein's college friend and recent addition to End of the Line, worked with Rein's growing construction business. He'd married End of the Line's music teacher, Sally Andersen, this past year and the two were presently awaiting twins sometime after Christmas—or so they hoped.

"Guess I didn't get as much sleep as I usually do," Rein confessed, not adding that "alone time now" came later than usual, which also meant the alarm went off much earlier.

"I've been reading up on raising kids." Clay tapped the base of the cabinet with his boot, shoring it against the wall. He shook his head. "Man, it makes this" --he gestured to the construction mess--"look like a piece of cake." He eyed Rein. "Caring for someone else's kid, I can't imagine what that's like."

"We've made some adjustments, but he's a great little guy," Rein replied. Cody had indeed been an unexpected addition to their lives at a time when he and Liberty were in the business of trying to have a family. They'd gotten the green light from the doctor after Liberty lost a child at four months. Their hopes had been dashed since with a false positive reading. A believer that practice makes perfect, he and Liberty had become creative with their lovemaking. Hot. Spontaneous. Comparable to the torrid little summer fling they'd engaged in just after her arrival to the ranch a couple of years ago.

It was tough. But for his wife, he was up for it.

"True," Rein said as he removed the wrapping on another

cabinet. "But damn, son, if half the fun isn't getting there. Am I right?"

Clay chuckled. "I'm trying to remember, dude. About the closest I get to my wife these days is to rub her feet. Sex is out. Twins can come early anyway, I guess. Doc doesn't want to start any contractions too early."

Rein blew out a breath. "What we do to make our wives happy, eh?" He thought about Liberty at home, probably utilizing her quiet time to design the nursery for Clay and Sally. He pushed away the idea that it wasn't their own nursery, but one of these days it would be. "Come on, with any luck we can get the rest of these cabinets in today. The appliances are coming Monday and we'll have more help with Dalton, Wyatt, and Tyler next week."

Clay nodded. "We may just be able to knock this out for Betty's holiday opening."

Betty walked through the back room with Jerry at her side, leaning heavily on his cane. Thankfully, the mild stroke had only slowed his speech and a bit of dexterity on one side. He suffered only from tired legs if he stood too long. During the design planning, Betty had requested that Rein widen the walkways in the back to accommodate Jerry's aging. "I don't know what the future is going to bring," she'd told him. "But cooking is his life. He loves this café,' and he'll be at that griddle until he no longer can be."

To help keep Jerry cooking for years to come, Rein had designed and built a new two-level stove top and griddle able to be converted when necessary.

"It's looking wonderful. You boys have made my every Christmas wish come true." Betty swiped at her eyes as she scanned the new bakery's kitchen.

"When are your tenants due back home?" Rein asked, pointing to the apartment above the bakery. Clay had gone to pick up Hank a few days ago and they'd been staying out at the Kinnison Last Hope Ranch in one of the cabins until yesterday.

"Hank took Julie and the boys out to California to see some friends and to finalize a couple of things with the divorce," Clay said. Clay and Hank, friends since college when the two hung out with Dalton and Rein, had rescued Julie and her two young sons from a dangerous standoff with Julie's abusive ex. Convincing his sister to move to End of the Line and live on the ranch hadn't been difficult for Clay. With a relationship blossoming between Julie and Hank and her boys being happy in town, Betty, sensing an opportunity, offered Julie a position as manager of the new bakery. It appeared that his sister and his nephews were ready to put down roots and start a new life in End of the Line. In addition, every weekend since Julie's arrival, Hank had been bouncing back and forth between his job in Chicago and visits to End of the Line.

Betty poked her head in the new cabinets, clucking with delight at the progress that had been made.

"I guess they discussed the possibility of Julie and the boys going to Chicago over the holiday to meet his family," Clay said as he helped Rein lift a cupboard into place.

"Sounds pretty serious," Rein said. "Betty, can you hand me my drill, please?"

She handed him the tool. Concern was etched on her usual jovial face. "That boy's not going to steal my new manager away from me, is he?"

Rein set in two screws, allowing the cabinet to stay secure in place. He glanced at Betty and, after setting the drill down, took a sip from his travel mug that Betty had just warmed up with fresh coffee. He leaned against the counter. "Hank spends more time here than he does in Chicago. Besides, he knows how much Julie and the boys need family right now." He lifted his mug to Clay. "As long as the big guy is here, I imagine your new bakery manager isn't about to budge."

Clay grinned. "And with Sally due, she's already mentioned wanting to be around to help out."

Rein shrugged. "I'm thinking we're going to be helping Hank remodel a new house in town here before too long."

Clay rubbed a hand over his chin. "Hank's a good guy. He's been great to Julie and the boys."

"Are you having reservations about him?"

Clay shook his head. "I just want Julie to be sure. Hank's got that proverbial white knight thing going on. I don't want to see either of them get hurt."

Rein nodded. "You do remember the secret crush he had on your sister, right?"

"Yeah… yeah, I do. I saw it on his face the night I showed him a recent photo of her back at the Buckle Ball."

"They'll be fine. They're both level-headed adults, right?"

Clay's brow rose with his half-smile.

"Fine. Julie's level-headed. One out of two ain't bad." Rein grinned.

Betty smiled, folding her arms with a contented sigh. "All this talk of romance and all the new little people in town reminds me of your Uncle Jed at this time of year. Lord, that man loved Christmas like no one I've met—before or since." She frowned, appearing to reconsider. "Except maybe your sister-in-law Aimee."

Rein nodded. "That's a fact, --the woman does love Christmas."

"She has certainly changed Wyatt on the topic."

Rein chuckled as he returned to the cabinet. "I don't know what happened to him that winter when all those kids were stranded out at the ranch, but now he seems driven to fill that house with a herd of children."

"Liberty was telling me today at our meeting that Gracie's new infatuation with Christmas trees has inspired him to volunteer to find us the biggest and best tree to decorate the town square. We haven't had one in years."

Rein tossed a look at Clay. "Which means we best get our butts in gear, because my brother is going to need help with this task and I'm fairly certain who he plans to ask."

A slow bass beat thumped out the first notes of Tone-Loc's "Wild Thing," and Rein scrambled to wrench the phone from his pocket. He caught Betty's shocked expression and Clay's half smile. "It's my wife. Sorry, got to take this."

"I certainly hope so," Betty muttered as she shooed Jerry back to the restaurant.

"Hey, I'm going to run home and check on Sally," Clay said, slipping into his work jacket. "I'll be back in fifteen minutes or so."

Rein sent him a nod of approval. "Hey, sweetheart, how's your day going?" he said into the phone.

"It's so quiet. I almost called Ellie to see how things were going, but I resisted."

Rein glanced at his watch. It wasn't even noon. The plans were to meet Ellie at the diner around six. "Hey, you could go get started on that bookshelf we designed for the nursery. I've got the pieces cut, but it needs a good sanding before we put it together. That might help pass the time." The seductive sound of her ring tone teased his brain, inspiring thoughts of how else they could spend the quiet time. Empty house. Gorgeous wife. A noon quickie....

"You're right, there's plenty to do. Sorry for the whine. I guess I've gotten used to little boy noise around here."

"I'd offer to come home and make some big boy noise, darlin', but I'm afraid I wouldn't want to come back to work."

"Big boy noise," she repeated, dropping her voice low.

The seductive tone shot straight below his belt. "I like big boy noise," she purred.

"Liberty," he warned with a grin that slowly curled his lip. He glanced around to make sure no one was within earshot. They'd played this game before and with incredible success.

"Honey, I don't want you to worry about me all alone out here," she continued. "I'm just being lazy. Lying here on the couch in my yoga pants and one of your old flannel shirts that smells like you." She chuckled.

His cock twitched.

"I'm hardly what you'd consider a bad boy's fantasy."

His body grew tense as he conjured the image of her doing a private dance for him. When it came to sex—phenomenal sex—she knew what buttons of his to push. He eased himself behind a stack of cabinet boxes. "What are you wearing under that flannel shirt?" His heart sped up when he heard her sigh.

"Why don't you come home and find out?"

Her voice pulled at his crotch. He squeezed his eyes shut, fighting the urge to unzip his pants and engage in a little old-fashioned phone sex with his wife.

Nope, not today. These little swimmers were currently a precious commodity. "I'll be home in ten… make that eight minutes, which gives us about fifteen minutes before lunch break is over." He was already walking toward the alley where his truck was parked. "I want you naked, wet, and ready for me, understand?" He saw Clay coming down the alley. "Be right back," he called out. *Got a baby to make.* Rein heard a sigh and pressed the phone to his ear as he climbed in the cab. Shit. "Don't get too far ahead of me, sweetheart." He disconnected and dropped the phone on the seat as he sped out of the alley, his mind decidedly on one thing and one thing only.

Seven minutes and a few seconds later, he raced through the front door. He dropped his coat in the foyer and unbuttoned his shirt as he searched the family room, finding it empty. He eyed his boots, thinking there wouldn't be time as he strode into the kitchen and found it, too, empty--though he eyed the sturdy kitchen island with a renewed perspective. His office was empty and so, too, the laundry room. He came down the hall next to the stairs and unbuckled his belt, ready for the hunt as he took the steps two at a time. "Liberty?" He stuck his head in their bedroom and found it vacant.

Walking down the hall, his pants unzipped, he called out, "Ms. Liberty Belle, your hunk of burning love is requesting to climb aboard—"

Liberty walked out of Cody's room, her eyes opening wide at the sight of his bulging manhood tenting his boxer briefs. Right here was as good as any place in the house. He hooked his thumbs in his belt loops, ready to get this show on the road.

"You didn't get my text?" she hissed in a frantic whisper. She stepped up to him and hastily fastened the snaps of his shirt.

Confused, he couldn't understand why she didn't want to see his hunk of burning love.

"What an unexpected surprise, honey," she said aloud. "You're here just in time to meet Mrs. Connors from Social Services. She stopped by to take a look at Cody's living arrangements. I was just showing her the bed you'd made."

Quick to zip his pants, he had just buckled his belt when a short woman with dark hair cut blunt across her small shoulders and wearing a suit the color of a sick flamingo emerged from the room. She was otherwise occupied, making a note on her clipboard, allowing Rein to fasten the last snap of his shirt. He smiled as she peered at him over the reading glasses perched halfway down her nose. She assessed him with the look of a mildly interesting science experiment.

"Mrs. Connors, this is my husband Rein."

The woman offered her hand, but her expression remained stoic. "Is it commonplace that you'd be home in the middle of a workday, Mr. Mackenzie?"

He eyed the woman. "Um… not really. As it happens, I'm on break and thought I'd come home and have my wife for lunch… have lunch with my wife, I meant to say."

The woman's brows shot straight through her blunt-cut bangs. "I see." She glanced at Liberty. "You mentioned that the child is visiting his mother today and is under Miss Harrison's supervision?"

"Yes, ma'am." Liberty nodded as she followed the woman down the stairs to the front door.

Rein tucked in his shirt, noticing the woman didn't miss a beat as she stepped over his coat.

"We're to meet at the diner later to pick him up. He loves the cinnamon buns." Liberty shot him pointed glances, no doubt suggesting he find a way to hide the bulge in his jeans.

He smiled as he placed his hand on the stair rail and crossed his boots. Despite Liberty's attempt to hide what was going on, Rein and the ostentatious woman had a silent understanding.

"Very well." She looked at Rein. "You should know that from time to time an agency representative may stop in unannounced. It is policy."

Rein smiled. *As it is my policy to make love to my wife in the middle of the day if I wish.* "Absolutely, Mrs. Connors."

Liberty appeared as though she might kill him as she walked the woman to the front porch. He came up behind her, placing his hand on her shoulder.

"Enjoy your lunch," Mrs. Connors said, waving as she climbed into her car.

Rein waved back. "Nice to have met you, Mrs. Connors. I shall."

He pulled Liberty inside before the woman was barely out of the drive and pushed her against the door. A groan uttered from her throat as she reached up and unsnapped his shirt.

"This is the strangest foreplay we've ever had," he said, capturing her mouth in a hot, wet kiss. He felt her fingers working at his belt as he reached beneath the hem of her shirt and sighed.

"Just as I thought—wearing nothing." He helped himself to a slow caress. "We aren't going to make it to the couch, you know that." He leaned his forehead to hers.

"Right here. Right now." She reached up and nipped at his lower lip as she curled her arms around his neck.

"Hell, yeah, and this is going to give you something to think about the rest of the day." He tugged her yoga pants down, helping her kick them away as he shoved his jeans past his hips. Lifting her, he entered her swiftly, finding her ready for him.

"It's your ring tone," he said, pressing deeper. "Wild thing describes you, sweetheart. It got me hard just talking to you."

She chuckled, burying her face in his neck, clinging to his shoulders as she moved with him. She whispered things he might not remember, but--as they toppled together into pure bliss--how she responded, how she fit him perfectly reminded him how much he loved this woman with every fiber of his being.

Between brief kisses and quiet laughter, they redressed.

"I'm late. I've got to get back to work," Rein said, tapping her nose with a grin. "But I'd like to thank you for lunch."

She licked her lips. "I'll see you at the diner."

Yeah, he could do this all over in a heartbeat. He picked up his coat and welcomed the chill in the air.

Chapter Three

R EIN HUGGED HIS WIFE. "HEY, we did it."
Liberty gazed up at him. She couldn't love this man any more than at this very moment. They stood together amid hundreds of area residents who'd come out on this frosty night in December to see the lighted parade and kick off the holiday shopping season in End of the Line. Cody sat perched on Rein's shoulders, taking in the wonder and beauty of the eighteen-foot Fraser fir lit entirely with old-fashioned colored lights. Every business surrounding the courthouse square was outlined with tiny white lights, and those businesses off the square had joined in celebrating the resurrection of the town lighting. The Git and Go, Tanners Meat Market, the bowling alley, Dusty's Bar and Grill, even the fire station and Doc Johnson got on board, outlining their buildings with white lights.

Wyatt held Gracie as he flipped on the generator he'd bought to offset electric expenses to the nearby courthouse. His face as he watched his daughter's joy was nothing short of a Christmas miracle.

"Good Lord." Betty sniffed. "I never thought I'd see the day," she said as she observed the sight.

"Ding, dong the Grinch is dead," Dalton said, tossing a grin to Betty. The Kinnison clan had designated the bakery as a sensible meeting spot to watch the parade. Dalton nudged his daughter's shoulder and pointed out that it'd started to snow. The two occupied themselves with catching snowflakes on their tongues.

"He may never grow up," Angelique commented as she snuggled with baby Sawyer under a blanket, watching her husband and daughter.

Liberty chuckled. "Isn't everybody a kid at this time of year?" she asked, watching her stepbrother.

Rein laughed. "In particular, that one." He nodded toward Dalton, who stood with his arms spread wide, face upturned, mouth wide open.

Beneath the gargantuan tree, Reverend Adam Bishop, newly appointed pastor at the Trinity Lutheran church, led the combined voices of his church and that of Reverend Leslie Cook's choir from the First Church of Christ in several secular holiday songs as well as tossing in a couple of holiday hymns. Reverend Cook, still fairly new to the area, was End of the Line's first female pastor.

"I'm glad to see the two church choirs joining forces," Betty remarked. "Maybe it will make things a little easier for Pastor Cook and the old-timers who don't seem to realize that women can be as committed to God and church as any man."

"I'm just glad that you all were able to convince the businesses in town to resurrect this tradition," Rein said.

"You all know this was originally Jed's idea," Betty said as she passed around a tray of cocoa and mini holiday cupcakes. "He would've loved to have seen you boys involved with your families like this."

The town lighting had kicked off just after dusk and the lighted holiday parade with participants from surrounding small towns as well as a school marching band from Billings was slated to begin in a few minutes.

Betty with her sparse but newly opened bakery had been handing out samples of her Snickerdoodle cookies, mini holiday cupcakes, and hot chocolate since just after the supper crowd at the café. This event was one of the very few times Jerry and Betty closed the café in the early evening--and only for one hour, and then it was back to work in case any of the holiday revelers wished to get a bite to eat before heading home.

"Where are Rebecca and Michael?" Liberty asked.

"He was asked to pull the trailer bed for the Crow nation entry," Angelique replied. "Aunt Rebecca wanted Emilee to dance, but this was her first parade and I wanted us together as a family."

Rein nodded. "It's a good thing. Someone has to keep an eye on Dalton." He lifted Cody off his shoulders, placed him in Liberty's arms, and kissed his sister-in-law on top of her head. "You're a saint, Angelique." He gave Liberty a quick kiss. "Try to save me one of those holiday cupcakes."

She grabbed his coat sleeve and kissed his cheek before whispering in his ear, "There are so many uses for icing."

He turned his face so they were nose-to-nose. "Do you want Santa to think you're a naughty girl?" he asked quietly.

She lifted a brow and smiled.

Rein shook his head. "You're killing me." He turned his attention to Cody. "You be a good boy" he said, kissing him on the cheek. "See you all later." He waved and disappeared through the throngs of parade-watchers.

Accepting a chair from Dalton, who'd been positioning camp chairs for everyone, Liberty sat down with Cody on her lap and covered their legs with an afghan she'd brought along.

Wyatt came walking across the main street now starting to line with crowds of people sitting in camp chairs and on blankets to watch the parade. "What'd I tell you?" He held his hand up to get a high five from Dalton. "Do I deliver or what?"

A little girl pointed at Wyatt. "Mommy, is that the man you called the Grinch?"

"The Grinch doesn't live around here anymore, sweetheart," she woman said, then smiled and tugged the little girl down the street.

Aimee joined her husband, hugging him and Gracie at once.

"It's a fine tree, Wyatt," Jerry said slowly as they walked by. He was seated in a lawn chair, with a blanket over his lap. "Jed would be delighted that our holiday traditions are back," he said, struggling to enunciate his words.

Wyatt stopped and shook the man's hand. "Thanks, Jerry."

"It's too bad that Clay and Sally can't be here. I know Sally would love this," Angelique said to her friends now seated together along the curb. Sawyer made a soft sigh and settled deeper into her arms, fast asleep despite the noise around him.

"I stopped over to take them a casserole tonight and she just seems miserable. I'll be very surprised if she makes it to January," Aimee said, accepting Gracie from Wyatt. He stood behind his family, seemingly taking in the whole scene as though for the first time.

Dalton had taken a spot on the curb beside his daughter as they waited for the parade to begin.

"Where's daddy?" Cody asked around a mouthful of cookie.

Aimee caught Liberty's gaze and smiled.

"He's helping some people with the parade, sweetheart. We'll see him afterwards." Liberty mentally applauded herself for sidestepping that, in all likelihood, Rein was in the Trinity Lutheran Church changing into his Santa gear and getting ready to bring up the end of the parade in the decked-out Kinnison horse-drawn sleigh. They'd found Jed's old Santa suit at the ranch after the fire, and decided to keep it and get it cleaned. She remembered the scene when Wyatt and Dalton had brought it over earlier in the week…

"Figured you'd be needing this." Dalton hung the red suit, complete with black Stetson, over the kitchen bar stool. "The owl was sitting on the woodshed when we drove in."

Rein looked up from the copy of *A Cowboy's Christmas* that he'd laid out to give Wyatt. "Good, then you can take this. Figure you'll want to read it at the open house Aimee mentioned the two of you are having."

Wyatt scratched his cheek and glanced away. "We'll have to see about it being an open house this year. Maybe we'll start out with family and a few friends."

Liberty offered coffee to the three most important men in her life—her husband and her two stepbrothers. "You all don't mind if I continue on with supper here, do you?"

"I don't know, what are you making?" Dalton asked, coming to stand beside her at the stove. He looked over her shoulder. "What the hell is that?"

"It's called broccoli cheese chowder and it happens to be Rein's favorite."

Dalton shook his head and sat down at one of the breakfast stools. "I always knew he was a little bubble short of plum."

Rein checked for Cody, and gave Dalton the finger.

"So, has he spoken to you?" Wyatt asked.

Rein glanced from Dalton to Wyatt. "The owl?"

"Jed," Dalton said, calmly folding his hands. "You know he's spoken to each of us."

Rein frowned and sat back, scratching his brow.

"I've seen the owl around here several times," Liberty offered. She sat down and watched the expressions of the three men. Did they really believe that Jed could speak to them from the dead? Michael Greyfeather's belief based in his Crow culture and religion was one thing—asking for Rein to believe it was quite another.

Her husband gave her a quick side look, then focused on turning the coffee mug between his hands. He shook his head.

"Yeah?" Dalton remarked, taking a swallow from his cup. "I wouldn't worry about it. Maybe things have gotten to the point where he feels it's not necessary." He finished his coffee. "Need to pick up a few things before I go home." Dalton eyed Rein. "We've been through a lot, the three of us. I'd like to think that Jed is happy with the way things are going. That we've done well continuing his legacy— the cabins, the Last Hope ranch, the equine rescue—and now bringing back the holiday traditions in town that he started."

Rein chuckled quietly. "At least he's assured of his line being carried on through you two."

Liberty felt her heart squeeze. She'd never seen Rein like this. She felt partly to blame that they hadn't yet had any children of their own. She touched his arm.

Wyatt spoke first. "Rein, you're his blood. We're adopted. Remember that. Besides, you know that legacies are about more than having children."

She knew what Wyatt intended, but also knew how important having children was to her and Rein.

"Yeah, you keep telling me that. It's easier when you already have kids, though, right?" He sighed and shook his head. "Hey, I hear what you're saying and I appreciate it. And I do feel good about all we've accomplished together."

"And man, I've never seen anyone as good with a kid than you are with Cody," Dalton said.

He met Dalton's gaze. "For as long as we have him."

Dalton blew out a sigh. "Give it some time. I know it's going to happen for you guys. I believe that, I really do."

"Like you believe Jed talks to you?"

Wyatt's gaze met Dalton's.

Liberty knew that things could turn ugly any moment. "It's been a long day. Cody's going to be waking from his nap soon. Maybe we could table this discussion for another time?"

Wyatt stood. "Thanks for the coffee." He looked at Rein and slapped his shoulder. "I'll bring the team to the church on Thursday."

Rein nodded, and amiable handshakes followed.

Liberty went back to the stove and allowed Rein time to mull over his thoughts. The strain of the bakery project deadline combined with sharing the duties of having a child in the house had taken their toll this week—on them and their lovemaking.

"It sounds stupid, but do you think there is some reason Jed seems more interested in Wyatt and Dalton?"

She stuck a pan of biscuits in the oven and turned, wiping her hands on a towel. "Baby, I don't know that I believe this idea that Jed's spirit is in this owl, or that he somehow spoke to Wyatt or Dalton. I never met him. What I know of him is what I've learned from the three of you, and what folks in town say about him. It seems that most people had a great respect for your uncle, and, more importantly, it seems to me that he loved the three of you a great deal."

He nodded. "What with the holidays and seeing that old Santa suit, and hearing about Jed's sage advice through some means I don't even understand..." he trailed off, sounding pensive, then shrugged. "I guess it made me realize that he was forced to take me in. He was the only family I had. You know, maybe having three boys to raise was too hard for him."

Liberty held up her hand. "Okay, you can stop there." This was not the behavior of her otherwise confident and too-often cocky husband. "Don't you dare say such things. You ask anyone in town and they'll tell you how he felt about you three boys. Good Lord, hasn't Betty sung the praises of you three enough times?" She leaned on the island and looked across the counter at him. "Don't you see? He had no children of his own. You three—you are his legacy."

"Daddy?" Cody called from the top of the stairs.

Rein pushed away his coffee cup and stood. "I'll go see to Cody. How long is supper going to be?"

"Another thirty-forty minutes." As she finished making supper, she wondered what Jed would have thought of her. Would he have been supportive of the fact that the daughter of his ex-wife, the woman who'd abandoned Wyatt and Dalton to Jed's care had gone and married Rein, his one and only relative by blood?

She looked out the kitchen window, startled by the streak of white flying through the twilight sky. She knew it was that damn owl. "So, talk to him already. What's it going to take?"

"Woo-hoo!"

The sound of Emilee cheering as she stood jostled Liberty back to the present. The short rasp of the End of the Line fire truck signaled the beginning of the parade.

For the next hour she watched as Dalton and Wyatt helped the kids collect the candy thrown to the curb and handed out by people dressed as elves and candy canes.

Cody clapped and giggled, delighted by the colored lights and holiday music blasting from the various homemade floats.

But nothing stirred her heart more than when Emilee pointed down the street and cried," It's Santa!"

Cody wiggled from her lap, and she followed him to the curb. He looked up, raising his arms, his smile unstoppable. Lifting him up, she watched the excitement of the crowd as they welcomed the horse-drawn sleigh. They'd had to add substantial padding around Rein's midsection, but he looked every bit the part with his white beard and black Stetson. He waved at the crowd, taking special notice of the children as he bellowed a deep "ho-ho-ho." Tears pricked at the back of Liberty's eyes and she glanced up, having only skated on the fringe of faith her entire life, and said a silent prayer that if any man deserved to be a father, it was this one.

"It's Santa!" Cody squealed, clapping his hands with glee.

"That's right, Cody."

His little hands clamped her face as he looked at her with eyes wide in wonderment. "He looked right at me and waved."

"I saw that, sweetie. He looked right at you. He must think you're a very good little boy." She hugged him.

He pushed back in her arms and studied her with a frown. "Will he know if I'm not at Miss Ellie's?"

"Santa knows everything, sweetheart. Of course he'll know where to find you."

Satisfied with her answer, he hugged her neck.

"Careful, don't get soap near his eyes."

Rein glanced up as Liberty placed a warm towel within his reach.

"Why is everything so wet? Let's try to keep it in the tub,

gentlemen."

He picked up the shampoo bottle and squinted at the tiny print. "Nate said this one didn't sting eyes." From the corner of his eye, he noticed Cody taking aim with the plastic water pistol he'd also picked up at the drugstore.

"You two have been up here for over an hour. I'm surprised he isn't wrinkled as a prune." She turned to leave as Cody fired. Rein ducked to one side and he felt a drip of water whizz past his ear. He watched in amazement as it stuck Liberty square in the back.

"Oh, buddy, you're in trouble now," Rein cautioned quietly as he filled up the second water pistol he had concealed beneath the sudsy water.

Cody's laughter echoed through the bathroom as Liberty turned slowly and fisted her hands on her hips. Rein gave her credit for trying to look angry, but he'd seen that glint in her eye before.

"You two are dangerous." She laughed as Cody squirted the side of Rein's face.

He glanced at the boy and smiled. It was a guy thing. "One, two--"

"Rein Mackenzie!" Liberty issued a stern warning.

He grabbed her ankle and held her in place as he unloaded the water pistol on her. Cody joined in, his laughter lightening the earlier heaviness in Rein's heart.

"You rats!" Liberty screamed. "Two against one isn't fair." She struggled, twisting to get to the sink, where she dumped a towel under the water. After soaking it, she slapped it down over Rein's head, much to Cody's unmitigated joy. "Playtime is over, cowboy," she said through her laughter.

He pulled the sodden towel off his head and checked the front of his T-shirt, which was pretty much a lost cause. "Okay, buddy, she's right. It's been a long day and it's time for bed."

Since his arrival Cody had spent nearly every moment with Rein or Liberty. He'd gone with Rein on errands. He'd met Nate at the drugstore where he'd had his first Green River at the soda fountain. They'd gone to the Git and Go where they'd shared a cherry slushy. They'd even been able to squeeze in a matinee at the movie theater. All firsts for Cody, it seemed, and for Rein a joy he hadn't experienced in years.

The sullen little boy who'd at first seemed quiet and shy had blossomed into a happy little boy under their care.

Tomorrow would be their first Sunday supper with the family, what with it being postponed the last couple of weeks due to work, illness, and the like. Though Cody had been around members of his family, this was another first—everyone at once. Rein hoped that his family would accept Cody as one of their own.

After reading the book about the magical dragon who'd befriended a little boy at least three times through, Cody had finally fallen asleep.

Rein watched him sleep. There was so much he should be thankful for, but he feared losing the people he loved. His Parents. Jed. Their unborn son. And one day, Cody. Hearing the sound of water splashing in the master bath, he smiled. He had Liberty. He had his health. She had hers.

He leaned against the master bathroom door, smiling at his beautiful wife soaking up to her neck in a tub of bubbles. "Hey, thanks for being a good sport about those water pistols. Impulse buys."

She returned his smile. "You're getting used to this dad thing, aren't you?"

He shrugged and sat down on the edge of the tub, letting his hand drift lazily through the sudsy water. "I guess so. You going to tell me that the 'mom' thing doesn't get to you just a little bit?" His fingertips brushed her knee. He loved when she sighed at his touch.

"He's only been here less than a month and already he's set up a permanent spot in my heart." She glanced at him, those eyes he adored shimmering with concern. "What am I going to do when he has to leave?"

"Whoa, slow down, sweetheart." He patted her knee. "One day at a time, okay? Think of it as a training ground."

"Is that how you do it?" She tossed him a curious look.

"Do what?"

"Manage not to get emotionally tangled up in all of this." He smiled. "I don't know if that's true." He stood to empty his pockets before peeling off his clothes and easing into the frothy bubbles. "I nailed it with this oversized tub, didn't I?"

"You're invading my space," Liberty stated with an arch of her brow.

"Oh, sweetheart, I haven't even begun my invasion of your space," he said, running his hands up the sides of her calves. "I don't believe I've formally tested the sturdiness of that two-sink vanity you had to have."

Liberty leaned forward and cupped his face with her wet hands. "Why do you think I was so insistent?" She brushed her lips to his with a smile, then met his mouth in a fiery kiss that led to yet another water mess to clean up.

Sometime later, after the structural validity of the vanity had been fully tested, they lay together in the dark, listening to the radio. Rein figured that Thomas Rhett had it right when he sang about being able to die a happy man. If this woman was to be his family, he'd gladly live with that. He hummed softly to the tune, languid in his thoughts, glad to be alive, here and with Liberty.

Her fingers traced concentric circles on his stomach, as always awakening his desire. "Did that bubble bath help to relax you, darlin'?"

She made a soft sound of approval. "Among other things," she said, sliding her leg against his.

The north wind outside howled through the tall pines beyond the clearing of their yard. Another Christmas was upon them and with all the chaos of getting the bakery done and Cody's arrival, he hadn't yet had time to go shopping for her. "You know, Christmas is coming up. I happen to have an in with the guy in the red suit. You thought about what you'd like to ask for?"

He drew her close, letting his hand rest on her hip. They'd grown accustomed to wearing pajamas in bed now to guard against being caught unawares. Still, the long gown she wore teased his mind knowing she wore no panties beneath. Rein turned to breathe in the scent of her hair, his hand caressing her hip.

"Have you thought about what you want?" she asked, tapping his chest with her finger.

The song he'd heard earlier—the one that rang so true in his heart—played in his head, even though the radio had moved on to a new tune. "Sweetheart." He kissed the top of her head. "I have everything I need, right here." He kissed the top of her head.

"So, I should take back the Rolex?" she teased. Her cheek flexed against his chest with her grin.

"Yeah, and you can cancel that trip to Paris while you're at it." He shifted to his side, holding her gaze as he ran his fingers down her cheek. "Honestly, Liberty, what more do I need? To hell with need. What more could I possibly want than what I already have?"

She pressed his hand to her cheek and kissed his palm.

Guilt for how he'd behaved the other day in front of his brothers surfaced, nudging his conscience. He'd said things in front of Liberty while wrapped up in his pity-party about not having a linage, and he'd been blind to how it might have sounded to his wife. "Baby, I'm sorry for how I behaved the other day with Wyatt and Dalton. I was feeling sorry for myself and I wasn't thinking about you—us—and everything we have together."

Liberty silenced him with her finger to his lips. "It has been a stressful time, Rein, and if trying to have a child right now is adding to that stress, we can wait."

He pulled her into his arms. "Listen, I want a child as much as you and I don't mind being determined about getting there." He grinned. "But I want you to understand, if—and I mean if—there is some unknown reason that we don't have kids of our own, I'd like to adopt. Maybe five or six."

She sat up and looked at him. "Five or six?"

"Too many?"

She smiled. "I can't recall that we've even discussed numbers. We've been so busy just trying to have one."

He stroked her bare arm. "I guess what you said made a lot of sense. Look at Wyatt, Dalton, and me. We were raised by a single rancher. No mother figure, unless you count Betty's watchful eye. And I think we turned out okay." He pulled her down into his arms. "Besides, how lucky could a kid get to have a mom like you?"

She rested her forehead against his chest, then looking up, searched his eyes. "But you do think we should keep trying, right?"

"Good Lord, woman, there isn't any place I'd rather be than here with you—day and night." He held her face. "All I'm saying is that whatever happens—whether we have ten kids of our own or adopt that many—or whether we'd decide it's just going to be you and me out here. Either way, I'm a happy man."

"Just when I think I can't love you more," she said, "you raise the bar."

Her lips found his and he locked his arm around her waist, the other sneaking beneath her gown, finding the warmth of where she straddled him.

She reached between their bodies and eased her hand into his boxer shorts.

"What are you doing there, darlin?" he asked, grabbing the headboard with both hands as he watched her bunch her gown around her hips. She freed him from the confines of the Ninja Turtle boxers he'd found that matched a pair for Cody. Incentive to get potty-trained, he'd explained to Liberty.

"What was it Doc told us? Patience and—" She took him in fully, bracing her hands on his chest.

"Dee-termination," Rein said with a groan of pure pleasure. He lifted his hips, pushing deep. "Oh, yeah, I like your determination, darlin'."

"Then you can tell Santa…" she said, moving her body with his.

Holding onto her thighs, trying to keep up nearly made Rein's eyes cross.

"That all I want for Christmas is…" A gasp tore from her throat.

There was something different about this time. He felt it as he rose, pushing deep, giving her everything—his heart, his body, his future.

"Is you, sweetheart," she sighed. "Just you."

Chapter Four

PER THE JUDGE'S ORDERS, CODY had gone every Friday afternoon with Miss Ellie to visit his mother for a few hours. Each time had proved to be more difficult in terms of his behavior when he returned to them. It was as though his demeanor had changed. Sullen, quick-tempered, aggressive—he usually took a nap, preferring to be alone until he was ready to be social. Liberty had brought it up to Ellie when she met them at the diner that Friday. "I know you said to expect some changes, but it seems to be getting worse," Liberty said to Ellie after buckling Cody into his car seat. "Is there any reason why? Something we should be more aware of?"

Ellie glanced at the car and sighed. "His mother made him a promise that she'd be out before Christmas and that they would spend it together. Today, however, she seemed preoccupied. She seemed hypercritical of Cody—his hair, his clothes, how he spoke to her, and then would tell him how much she missed him. Mixed messages."

"We've been trying to teach him to use his manners. We're not trying to overstep anything."

Ellie patted her arm. "I doubt that teaching a child a few manners is going to harm anyone." She shrugged. "As long as they are basic manners that anyone would teach, I think you should go ahead, just as you're doing."

"Sunday is a family dinner over at Wyatt and Aimee's. Do

you think it's too much to force him to be social?"

"You can see," she replied. "But honestly, I think he needs family. Children tend to respond favorably when they're welcomed into an environment of love and acceptance."

Liberty nodded. "Taking my cues from you, Ellie," she said, accepting Cody's backpack.

"There is something you need to know. Rowena's lawyer is trying to get enough collected to post her bail before Christmas. And, I've heard something about a plea bargain. If that should happen, there's a good chance she'll get Cody back." Ellie stated. "That said—I've made the offer that she and Cody are welcome to live at the house, with the caveat that she get a job and keep her nose clean."

Liberty realized for the first time the weight that Ellie placed on her own shoulders when it came to caring for and helping these displaced families.

"It's a gamble," she said, "but I'd rather have her living in the house so my staff and I can keep an eye on Cody.

Not thrilled by the news, Liberty headed home, knowing Rein would be even less enthralled. When he arrived home that evening after helping Nate with some renovations at the pharmacy, Cody was still in his room.

Rein dropped his tool belt over the hook by the back door. He gave her a kiss and glanced in the family room. "Where's Cody?" He narrowed his gaze. "Did he come back the same as before?"

Liberty nodded. "Yes, I'm afraid so, but there's more. It seems Rowena's lawyer is trying to strike a deal to get her three-month sentence reduced and post bail before the holidays. She's claiming she was a victim, that she didn't realize she was meeting up with a drug dealer, claiming that she thought it was a job interview her friend had set up for her."

Rein frowned. "Christmas is just a few days away."

"I know. His mom apparently implied strongly to Cody that they'd spend Christmas together. She made it sound like a done deal."

Rein leaned back against the counter and listened. His eyes focused on his boots.

"Has he been in his room since you brought him home?"

"He took a short nap," Liberty said. "When I checked on him a bit ago, he was sitting on the floor playing with the farm set."

Rein pushed away and sighed. "Maybe we should do a pizza and movie night? He likes those. We could watch that movie he likes. The one about the little fish that gets lost."

"Finding Nemo?" Liberty said. Her heart twisted thinking of just how many times they'd watched that movie, Cody's attention intently focused on the dynamic between the father fish and his son.

"Yep, that's it. Why don't you go ahead and place the order? Since the Git and Go got that new pizza oven, they've started a delivery service." He gave her a quick peck on the cheek. "I'll go talk to Cody." He paused, resting his hands on her shoulders. "Hey, it's going to be okay, sweetheart." He kissed her forehead.

Later that evening the three sat at the low coffee table in front of a roaring fire in the fireplace and watched the animated movie for what seemed like the hundredth time. They munched on Git and Go pizzas, delivered by a senior that Denise had hired over the holiday break. Liberty had managed to eat one slice of cheese pizza, while the other two annihilated the better part of the double pepperoni pizza they'd ordered.

Sunday ushered in a bank of low, steely-grey clouds as the three of them drove to Wyatt and Aimee's for noon dinner. To many in the community, it would always be known as the Kinnison ranch, named after the cattle baron who built and ran it for years. After his death, Rein had found his uncle's journal and realized that his Uncle Jed had wanted to make the ranch a place of second chances, of finding healing through hard work and nature. To set it apart, they'd dubbed it the Kinnsion Last Hope Ranch, to include the set of nine cabins that Rein, his brothers, and friends had constructed for the purpose Jed had intended. Ever since, they'd hosted both horses and individuals passing through End of the Line, as well as offering it as temporary housing to those in need. They'd started riding programs for kids with special needs, and nature outings for the families that lived at Miss Ellie's house in Billings.

Liberty hopped down from the truck, feeling better than she had a couple of nights before. She grabbed the cheesy potato casserole she'd made as her contribution to the meal, while Rein helped Cody from his car seat. Her eye caught the presence of the white owl seated amid the evergreen of the tall pine that grew between the house and what was once Rein's wood-working barn. Saved from the fire two years ago that damaged much of the back of the ranch, the tree remained a symbol of Kinnison longevity.

The wood-working barn now stored much of the furniture that Rein had built over the years. It was part of her's and Rein's future plans to open an online business for custom-made pieces crafted in the rugged, rustic style that represented their love of repurposing vintage pieces into modern-day usefulness.

She chose not to mention the owl to Rein. While earlier tensions seemed to have been resolved among the three brothers, they hadn't revisited the topic of Jed's alleged visitations to his brothers.

Michael Greyfeather, an old family friend of Jed's and now the head of the ranch's equine rescue mission, opened the front door to greet them. "Hey, guys, I saw you coming

and thought I could help out." He nodded toward the casserole. "Let me take that for you." He smiled at Rein and
then at Cody. "I don't think I've had the pleasure yet, young
man." He leaned down and held out his hand in greeting
to Cody.

Cody shied away, ducking behind Rein's leg.

Michael smiled and nodded. "I'll just take this in. Come
on, hang up your things. Everyone except Clay and Sally
are here."

Rein hooked his hat on the antler rack that hung in the
foyer. Cody stayed close to Rein's side.

Aimee smiled as she emerged from the kitchen and saw
them. Hugging them both, she smiled at the reclusive little
boy. "Hi Cody, welcome to our home."

"Can you say hi, Cody?" Liberty asked quietly.

Aimee smiled, giving Liberty a look that she understood
the boy's shyness. "It's great that we're all be together again.
It's been too long." She smiled. "Then again, I'm spoiled. I
love having everyone under the same roof."

Rein tossed Dalton a wave. He sat in Jed's old rocker near
the fireplace, cradling his son, Sawyer.

Wyatt hugged Liberty and then Rein. "Good to see you.
Dad would have been really pleased with how well the
parade went." He was referring cryptically to Rein's per-
formance as Santa.

"Guess we're lucky Santa was able to stop by with it being
so close to Christmas." Rein knelt down at Cody's side as
Sadie, the Kinnison's golden retriever, meandered over to
greet the new scent in the house. The dog, almost ten years
old now, showed signs of aging. Her brows and chin were
graying, her eyes less bright than they once were. Nonetheless, she continued to have approval of who entered her
house. She sniffed Cody's hand, bumping it with her cold
nose.

He jerked his hand away and pushed close to Rein. It startled the dog and she backtracked from the boy, unsure of his intent.

"Sadie won't hurt you, buddy. She's just smelling you. That's how she says hello."

Cody eyed the dog who waited patiently, her tail in jubilant motion as Rein reached out to smooth his hand over her head. "My Uncle Jed brought us Sadie when we were in high school, that was a long time ago. She's a good old dog. You want to pet her?"

Cody's jaw set firm. He shook his head.

"Sadie, come, get your supper, girl," Emilee called out, holding the dog's dish. Her dark braids fell over her slim shoulders. The young girl looked like her mother, Angelique, with her dark eyes and hair, but as she grew older it was Dalton's personality that she resembled most. Dutifully, the dog lumbered behind as they walked to the kitchen.

Cody released a small sigh.

A short while later, the large group sat around the massive dining room table. It had been built by Rein years before as one of his first furniture-making endeavors.

Liberty smiled as she had a flashback memory of her first meal at this table. Guarded, cantankerous, and more than a little rebellious, she'd just arrived from her former life as a dancer in a Vegas club. Wanting to escape her life, she'd found her half-brothers and requested sanctuary at the ranch until she could get on her feet.

"What are you thinking about?" Rein leaned over to ask quietly.

"Just thinking about my first morning here." She met his blue-eyed gaze. "Your critique of my outfit. How I put you in your place." She gave him a quick kiss. "I think I started falling in love with you that very moment, right here."

He returned the kiss. "I was an ass back then," he said

quietly so the kids couldn't hear.

"Back then?" Wyatt smiled as he leaned over to pass the potato casserole.

Rein narrowed his gaze on Wyatt and accepted the casserole.

"Your house looks beautiful," Liberty told Aimee.

"I agree, Aimee. This is a step-up from those paper snowflakes you tried to teach me last year," Angelique said with a laugh.

"I had to make them for her," Emilee interjected.

Aimee shrugged. "Wyatt actually did the majority of it. I was so busy on the town lighting committee that he got tired of waiting. I think" --she leaned over to give Wyatt a kiss--"he did a beautiful job."

Gracie clapped at the sight of her parents kissing.

"Cheap entertainment," Dalton muttered, then offered Wyatt a surprised look. "What?"

"Who are you and what did you do with my brother?" Rein asked Wyatt. "Aimee, you've worked miracles with this one."

"I know where you live, buddy," Wyatt joked.

Baby Sawyer lay in a portable crib placed near Dalton and Angelique. Emilee, unusually quiet this evening, sat between her mother and the Greyfeather's—Michael and Rebecca, who'd raised Emilee when her mom—their niece—was going through some tough times.

Liberty thought about all they'd been through in the short time she'd been in End of the Line. Yet, together—Dalton, Angelique, Wyatt, Aimee, Michael and Rebecca, Sally and Clay—they'd formed the bonds of a family. She dabbed at her eyes, damp from the unexpected emotions welling inside her. She was so grateful to have Rein, to be a part of this family.

Rein reached beneath the table and grabbed her hand,

giving it a squeeze. His smile showed his gentle concern. "You okay?"

She nodded. "Just not as hungry as I thought I'd be." She leaned back and took a cleansing breath. "I just need to slow down and enjoy."

Rein nodded and patted her leg.

"Has anyone heard from Hank?" Wyatt asked.

He had flown Julie and her boys to Chicago earlier in the week to meet his family and celebrate Christmas. They'd planned to be back here on Christmas Day to join in the gathering that Wyatt had planned. Several close friends, a few community members, and those in Rein's construction firm had also been invited.

"You know, I'm not trying to pour salt in a wound, but I feel kind of bad for Julie having to put up with Hank's sister," Liberty said.

"The woman needs to find a rich cowboy to take care of her."

"And hope that he has plenty of patience," Rein added with a shake of his head.

"Hey, if Wyatt can snag someone as good as Aimee, there's hope for Caroline Richardson." He tossed his brother a wicked grin and got beaned in the head by a dinner roll.

"Wyatt!" Aimee gasped. "Careful of what you're teaching your daughter."

He picked up a roll and held it up to Gracie. "No, sweetheart, this is how I'd teach my daughter." He leaned down and pointed to Dalton. "Toss this at your...I mean, to your Uncle Dalton. He's the furry one at the end of the table."

Before her mother could intercede, Gracie flung the roll and it landed no further than the end of her plate.

"We'll work on that arm, baby girl." Wyatt leaned over and kissed her chubby cheek.

"So, what do you have planned for this shindig, bro?"

Dalton asked as he calmly buttered the roll his brother had thrown at him.

Wyatt thought for a moment, and glanced at Aimee.

"Hey, as long as Betty and Rebecca bring the desserts and you guys handle the meat, I can provide the rest."

"Are you having a sleigh ride?" Liberty asked, taking a small bite of her casserole.

"Oh, that'd be fun. We could offer them in shifts."

"I could handle that," Michael stated. "Emilee can help me. She's good with the horses, like her mama." He grinned at Angelique.

"And you've got to read the story. That's tradition," Rein offered.

Wyatt nodded. "Yeah, remind me to talk to you about that." He pointed his fork at Rein.

The remainder of the meal was punctuated with laughter and stories and thoughts about where End of the Line was going as a growing community.

Liberty noted how Cody had picked at his meal, much as she had, but he'd been quiet, only speaking when spoken to and then offering only one-word responses.

After lunch, Liberty walked over to admire the beautiful live, eight-foot tree that Wyatt and Aimee had set up at the end of the great room. It stood in front of the majestic cathedral windows rebuilt to their former state, after the fire. In the daylight, they offered a spectacular view of the snow-capped mountains in the distance.

The tree was decorated with a few store-bought ornaments, but many were handmade by Aimee's former students. Emilee had been in her second grade class two years before when a blizzard had blown up during an unorthodox field trip to the ranch just before Christmas—back when most of the community had dubbed the reclusive Wyatt Kinnison "the Grinch." Still fighting the grief of losing her twin sister at the time, Aimee and Wyatt would fall in love in those few days they were stranded with children on the ranch.

Aimee walked up beside Liberty. "Hey, I wanted to ask you something."

"Sure." She kept an eye on Cody who'd gone around to the other side of the tree.

"Do I look any different?" Aimee asked.

Liberty studied her. "Different? How?"

Aimee leaned in close and whispered. "I took a home pregnancy test. It came back positive." She put her finger to her lips. "I'm not going to say anything to anyone else until I know for sure this time." She glanced at Liberty. "You remember that you called it with Gracie. Before even I knew. I just wondered if you noticed anything."

Liberty took Aimee's hand and squeezed it. "Has Wyatt cooked any bacon lately?"

Aimee frowned as though in thought. "No, he hasn't."

"I remember you turned green as a gourd at the scent of frying bacon. I can't say that it'd happen again, but that's when I first noticed."

A blood-curdling scream from the other side of the tree stopped Liberty's heart. She and Aimee darted around the tree and found Emilee, her hand over Cody's. Both were poised on a miniature John Deere tractor ornament.

Emilee's gaze was fixed on their hands. She seemed in a trance, unable to break free from whatever the child was seeing in her mind. Her dark brown eyes were filled with terror.

"Emilee?" Angelique rushed to her daughter and knelt beside her. Rebecca followed close behind. Both women knew that it was the young girl's gift as a 'seer' that produced these random events.

"She's seeing something. Be gentle," Rebecca cautioned.

Tears rolled down the little girl's face. Her head moved slowly side to side as though she didn't want to believe what she saw.

"Em, it's Mama, darlin'. I'm here, sweetheart."

Dalton also knelt next his daughter. "Em, dad's here. Come on back to us, baby."

Liberty had witnessed snippets of the young girl's ability to 'see' things in the past, but they'd never before been this pronounced, or this emotional.

Dalton laid his hand carefully over Emilee's, and, after a heartbeat, she looked up at him. Fat tears dropped from her eyes when she blinked. She grabbed Dalton around the neck and hugged him tight. Whatever she'd seen had clearly terrified her.

Cody stood still, his little chest heaving in and out with his labored breathing. If not calmed down, he'd most likely hyperventilate. Rein picked up the small boy and hugged him close, walking away as he whispered softly, trying to calm the child.

"I didn't mean to see it," Emilee sobbed into her father's neck. "I didn't mean to."

Rein suggested that maybe they should get Cody home and they'd call later to discuss what happened. Liberty drove home, with Rein, leaning back to hold Cody's hand the entire way.

Liberty wasn't hungry, but suggested cold pizza or soup she had in the freezer for Rein and Cody. She wasn't feeling well and decided to lie down, startled sometime later by the ringing of her cell phone. Angelique, calling to check on Cody.

Liberty glanced at the clock by their bed, and realized through her grogginess that she'd slept much longer than she'd anticipated. It was past Cody's bath time and well into getting ready for bed. She blinked to clear her head.

"Are you okay? You sound as though you were sleeping."

Liberty swallowed at the dryness in her throat. "I'm fine. Just a little tired. Cody's fine, I think. He's been with Rein since we got back home. How's Em?"

"She's better, but still pretty shaken up," Angelique said. "Let me be honest in saying I don't know much about this gift my Aunt Rebecca feels my daughter has. She says it comes from my great-grandmother—a full-blooded Crow shaman who had the gift of 'sight'."

"The child was terrified, Angelique. What in God's name did she see?"

There was a slight pause. Enough to cause Liberty to sit up and listen carefully.

"She described a room—she didn't know where, only that it seemed small. There were four or five people, male or female, she couldn't decipher," Angelique explained.

Thus far, it sounded more along the lines of the old, black-and-white scary movies that sometimes Em and her dad would watch together. Dalton was an avid fan of old horror movies, where most things looked staged and almost funny in comparison to modern horror films.

Angelique cleared her throat. "She saw a lot of blood—on the floor, the walls, and on the people."

"Like a murder scene?" Liberty asked, horrified that such a vision would have to be seen by anyone, much less a child.

"That upset her, yes, but what she screamed about was seeing Cody standing there. He, too, was covered in blood."

She dropped her feet to the floor and sat on the edge of the bed as Rein walked in the room. "Cody—was he?" She couldn't bring herself to say the word.

"She just said that he was standing in the room, and was screaming for his daddy."

Liberty's heart twisted. She felt bile rise in her throat.

"Has Cody ever mentioned a father? Does Ellie know if

there is one?" Angelique asked.

Liberty shook her head, jarring loose the disturbing image planted in her brain. "Um…I, no, she's never mentioned a father figure. You'd think if there was one that cared, he'd have shown up by now, wouldn't you?"

"Valid point," Angelique said, and then sighed. "I am going to tell them both no scary movies for a while—I don't care if Dalton calls them cheesy or not. I'm really sorry, Liberty, but we felt you ought to at least be aware of what Em saw."

"Thank you, I appreciate that. I'll call Ellie tomorrow and see if I can find out anything more." Her eyes rose to meet her husband's steady gaze. He was the only one she knew of that Cody would call "daddy".

∞

The next morning after Rein left to meet with Wyatt and Clay for breakfast at Betty's, Liberty waded through a load of laundry and two cups of coffee, fed Cody his breakfast, and then settled him on the couch in the family room with his favorite soft blue afghan to watch his sing-a-long videos.

She sat down, debating whether to call Ellie. Finally, she dialed her number.

"Hey, Ellie, it's Liberty. Got a minute?"

"Sure, is everything okay?"

Liberty hesitated, unsure of where to begin.

"Did the Sunday dinner thing go okay?" Ellie asked.

"It did… mostly. It was a relatively pleasant day. Cody picked at his food, stayed pretty quiet."

"Until?" Ellie prodded. "I can hear in your voice that something happened."

"You know Emilee Kinnison, my niece? Dalton's oldest."

"Yes, I've been around her many times since moving here.

Very mature for her age. A gifted child."

"That is true. And it seems her Grandma Rebecca feels that she may have the ability to 'see' things—visions, if you will. But they seem random at best. And it's unclear if they're past, present, or future."

"She did nail Sawyer's gender, even before Angelique knew."

"True, and I've seen it occur a couple of other times, but nothing of this magnitude. This was very different."

"How so?" Ellie prodded.

"Emilee was terrified and frankly, if I'd seen what she told her grandmother she saw, I'd be terrified, too."

"At the very least, concerned, I'd think."

"Exactly, and that's why I called. To find out if Cody has a father in his life somewhere. Maybe a boyfriend of Rowena's that he called 'daddy'?"

"No, not that I'm aware of. It was just the two of them when they came to us. She said they'd been traveling north from New Orleans, living pretty much from place-to-place, making their way to relatives in Canada. She had Cody's birth records with her and it didn't indicate a father. But as you know, many women who come through our doors are seeking safety from an abusive relationship. Has Cody been asking to see his dad?" Ellie asked.

"No," Liberty replied.

"What did Emilee say that she saw?"

"What she described sounded like a horrible accident, perhaps...there was a lot of blood." She paused to take a breath and glanced at Cody, seemingly unscathed by the incident and content as could be, enraptured by the video. "I'm not sure I understand this notion of seeing visions."

"Why don't you tell me the rest. What makes you ask about his father?"

"Angelique said that Emilee saw Cody standing over

these bodies. He was covered in blood and he was screaming out for his daddy," she finished, resting her palm to her forehead. "I don't know what to think."

There was a long pause. "Well, to my knowledge, Rowena has never been involved in anything even close to that type of incident. And I would hazard a guess that if she had been, Cody's behavior would be showing obvious signs of seeing something that traumatic."

Reason. "You're right, that makes sense."

Ellie cleared her throat. "Though that isn't going to make what I have to tell you any easier. In fact, I was just picking up the phone to call you when you rang through."

Liberty stilled. "What is it?"

"Rowena agreed to the deal. She gave them some names. The judge instructed her to do three hundred hours of community service and she received a one-year probation, as it was her first offense. She gets released later today."

"And Cody?" She could barely get out the question, knowing already the answer was one she'd effectively been sweeping under the rug for days now.

"He awarded Cody back to his mom."

Her brain went on shut down. How was this possible? Couldn't the judge see how unwise it was to send this little boy back into such uncertainty?

"Liberty?"

"Isn't there anything you can do?" Liberty asked, trying to keep her emotions on an even keel. "Do you feel this is the right thing—the best for Cody?"

"Listen, I know how hard this is. You and Rein are good people. But the fact is that our system is designed to keep mothers and children together if at all possible."

Liberty felt as though her heart had been ripped from her chest.

"She agreed to the terms I set. At least they'll be living

here--that's some comfort, I hope."

"So, the probation means she cannot move out of state, correct?" Liberty asked.

"That's true. However, she can still decide who Cody has contact with. Right now, that's a short list which includes me, the social worker, and one other staff member." Ellie released a sigh. "It's not ideal. Admittedly, I share your concern. But we've got to give her a chance to make things right by her son. And hopefully, she may agree to allow you some visitation."

"But his Christmas presents—Rein built him a little barn to go with his farm set." Liberty searched her mind, trying to remember where she'd hidden all the little gifts for him.

"You can wrap them and give them to me if you like. I'll see that he gets them."

Her eyes filled with tears. She bit her lip and breathed in deeply to keep from falling apart.

"I know what you're feeling, Liberty. I do. I've wanted to hang on to so many of the kids whom I've seen over the years. That's part of what we do, show love and family to kids who really need it. Sometimes, those kids are lucky enough to stay in those good homes, and other times their visits are short."

Tears began to roll down Liberty's cheeks.

"The system honestly needs more good, caring people like you and Rein, and I want to thank you from the bottom of my heart for that. Because of you, Cody was able to experience unconditional love and acceptance. Something I doubt he's had much of before now. But because I have seen people turn their lives around, I hope that his mom will be able to show her son that same kind of love. He won't forget you or the kindness you've shown him--of that, I'm certain."

"When will he need to be ready?"

"This afternoon," Ellie stated softly. "We can meet at the diner if you like, or I can come to your place. We can tell him together—with you and Rein, or we can treat it as though he's going on a visit to see his mom. Maybe it's best if I explain everything to him once we get back to Billings. It might be less painful for everyone. I'll come back up in a couple of days to check on you and get his presents."

Liberty's heart was about to break. "I'll pack his favorite toys and his clothes in his backpack."

"That would be very kind, thank you. Shortly after lunch, then?"

Liberty swallowed sorrow the size of a basketball down her throat. "Sure, that will give us some time this morning together."

"It's going to be okay, Liberty." Ellie said. "I'll see you after lunch."

Liberty wiped her nose and brushed her tears away as she noticed Cody getting up from the couch. "That's what Rein said."

Cody padded into the kitchen and looked at her. "Are you okay?" He hadn't often called her mom, but she'd felt the trust between them and had told him daily how much they loved having him in their lives.

"I'm okay, baby. Is your video done?" She took his hand and walked to the family room. "I feel like watching some more of these, how about you?"

He nodded with a big smile, climbed up onto the couch, and grabbed his blanket as he burrowed into a nest of throw pillows.

Liberty tucked herself in close and draped her arm over the back of the couch. Instinctively, he scooted close, snuggling beneath her arm.

"Is that girl, Emilee, going to be okay?" he asked quietly as the video began.

"That's very nice of you to ask, Cody. Yes, I think she's okay now." She brushed a wisp of his hair from his forehead. It's going to be okay. Maybe if she said it enough times, her heart would start to believe it.

☙❧

"How in God's name is this okay?" Rein paced the room, shaking his head at the sheer audacity of it all. He'd come home to find Liberty seated on Cody's bedroom floor, her eyes rimmed red from crying.

She rubbed the heel of her palm over her eyes. "We both knew this was going to happen. That's the way the system works."

"Yeah, well, the system" --he crooked his fingers into air quotes--"is fucked up. Isn't there anything Ellie could do?"

"She said that whenever possible, it's best to keep the mother and child together."

He stopped, his frustration beginning to wane in light of how his wife had suffered this afternoon. "You should have called me. Clay and I were just talking to Tyler after Wyatt left, and then Betty asked us to take a look at something she'd like to include in the kitchen." He looked down at where she sat by Cody's bed. "I'd have been here in a heartbeat, sweetheart, you know that."

"I know, and Ellie offered a number of ways to handle it. None of them sounded right, or easy. I was being totally selfish," Liberty said as she stood and realized how late it had gotten.

Rein followed her into their bedroom.

She placed her hand on the top of her head as though trying to control her thoughts. "I just sat with him… all morning, watching those silly videos he loves." Her voice sounded wounded—detached.

"I told Ellie we had his presents. She said she'd come up in a day or two and get them if we wanted. She'd make sure he got them."

"Did Cody understand he wouldn't be coming back?" Rein asked.

Liberty sat on the edge of the bed. "I packed his backpack with his favorite toys. I kissed him goodbye like I always do when he's going to see his mom. Which is technically true." She looked up, her tear-stained face stricken with concern. "I couldn't do it, Rein. I didn't know how to explain. Ellie said it was easier if she explained it to him once they got back to Billings."

He knelt in front of her. "It's okay, baby." He swallowed the lump in his throat. One of the reasons Wyatt had called the breakfast meeting was to ask him to play the role of Santa at the ranch holiday gathering. He'd been hesitant at first, feeling it should be Wyatt's duty as head of the Kinnison ranch. But it hadn't taken much to convince him to take on the job when he mentioned how Cody's face lit up the night of the parade.

"We should go ahead and give her the presents, don't you agree?" Liberty asked.

Her question jostled him from the memory of that night and the image of Liberty holding Cody, his tiny, red mittens waving wildly at Santa as he drove the sleigh--equipped with its summer wheels—down the street. He stood with a sigh and unsnapped his shirt, pulling it off his shoulders. It was probably better that he hadn't been around when Ellie came. He might have said things Cody shouldn't hear--and Ellie didn't deserve to hear. She was simply following protocol. Deep down, he knew it.

"I'm going to go to bed, I'm exhausted. We can deal with Cody's room tomorrow." Liberty came up behind him and wrapped her arms around his waist. She laid her cheek against his back. "You okay?"

He turned and pulled her into his arms. Holding her stabilized his emotions. "I will be." He rested his chin on the top of her head. "Wyatt asked me to play Santa at the holiday gathering."

She looked up, holding his gaze. "Sweetheart, you are one of the best Santa's I've ever seen, but Wyatt, of all people, would understand completely if you passed the baton to him or Dalton this year."

He breathed in deeply, then shook his head. "It'll take me a couple of days, but I'll do it. Em, Gracie, Julie's boys—they all deserve a happy Christmas, too." He managed a half-grin. "I guess we could all use a little magic in our lives right now."

She hugged him. "We'll get through this, right?"

He squeezed her tight. "We will. I love you, darlin'. I'll be up in a few minutes. I'm going down and checking the house."

"Don't be long," she called as he started down the steps.

Rein wandered through the house, checking doors, shutting off lights. He walked into the family room just off the kitchen and saw the dozens of video cases and DVDs strewn across the coffee table. At one end of the couch, the pillows had been piled together. The blue afghan that Cody dearly loved was tossed across them.

Weariness overcame him and he slumped down on the couch, staring before him at the array of music videos. He smiled as he remembered Saturday mornings when Cody begged for Rein to put one in—it didn't ever seem to matter which; any of them would do.

They'd been a recommendation from Sally, who said that her younger students loved them and even some of her older students would borrow them from time-to-time. Liberty had bought one online and Cody had loved it so much that she wound up buying the whole set.

He should put them away, tidy up things a bit, but the truth was he wanted to hang onto the chaos—it reminded him of Cody. Rein leaned back and reached for the blanket. He wadded it in his hands and held it close to his chest. A heavy loss, so much like when they'd lost their son last spring, washed over him. He pressed the blanket to his face and breathed in the little boy's scent that lingered in the soft fabric. Tears stung at the back of his eyes. How much more could he take? He fought the sob that finally broke free, tearing from his throat in a low anguish. He tossed the blanket aside and leaned forward, fighting the pain. He tried to put it in perspective, tried to remind himself that he'd known going into this that it was a temporary situation. He shook his head, the sorrow rising through him finally surfacing. He covered his face and let the tears come. And then, determined to be strong—for Liberty, for them both--he pulled in a deep breath and swiped his hands over his face. He sniffed, telling himself that things would be all right. And while he drank only on special occasions--and then only beer--he decided that tonight Jamison might be in order to help him sleep.

He found a glass and rummaged through the cabinet until he found the open bottle that had been there since they'd christened the house. He poured it half full, judging from what he could tell in the dark kitchen, and sat down at the kitchen island to leisurely sip the potent whiskey.

"Do you remember what I used to tell you boys when something went wrong at school?"

The voice in his head—most likely influenced by the generous gulp of Jamison he'd just swallowed—sounded so very much like his Uncle Jed. Rein shook his head. Damn, that sounded as though he was standing right here. He eyed the glass, thinking the Irish whiskey packed more of a punch than he remembered. "You mean," he said aloud, "like the time I got beaten to a pulp because Dalton mouthed off to the wrong kid and his brother took it out on me? Yeah, I remember."

"You aren't strong, son, just because you've been through some hard times."

"That, according to Dalton, is true." He lifted his glass to his solitude. "To his way of thinking I've not yet hit my stride of hard times." He tipped his head at the sudden thought. "Though it does beg the question, if I'm talking to myself and imagining you in my head, then I may have hit the payload of hard times at this exact moment."

"You're strong because of how you reacted to and over-came those difficult situations. Oh, hell, I'm preaching to the choir here."

Rein stared at the glass, remembering when the three of them had toasted Jed's memory after the funeral. Standing at his old desk, they'd polished off the remains of the Jamison they'd found in his uncle's liquor cabinet. Even then, Rein could still smell the scent of his uncle's Old Spice aftershave lingering in the library.

Kind of like now.

Rein sighed and polished off his drink, welcoming the slow burn down his throat.

"You've always had a great inner strength, Rein. Liberty knows it. She can depend on it. You're both going to need it. She's a good woman. I can't believe she's Eloise's kid. She's not a thing like her mom, thank your lucky stars."

He frowned. It was one thing to have memories so vivid of what someone dear once said to you, but quite another to have those memories reference the present.

"Is that really you?" he asked, scanning the dark house around him.

Outside the sound of an owl hooted twice, then all was

silent.

He looked around. "So, that's it, then?" Shaking his head, he stood and placed his glass in the sink.

"Not exactly."

The voice appeared again and Rein clung to the sides of the countertop. Outside, perched on the deck railing, sat the Great White Owl. He peered straight at Rein.

"I've wanted to thank you for helping bring my dream of the ranch to life. It means a great deal to me, son, that you set your sights on making it happen and brought your brothers up to speed with the idea. I'm proud that each of you had a hand in the process. You built a family, beyond the three of you. Tell Wyatt I'm glad to see Michael at the ranch. Listen to him, he's a good man, but don't work him too hard. He's not as young as he used to be."

"Uh…okay," Rein answered. Though he wasn't sure if it was the whiskey or the possibility that he was losing his mind. "This sounds like you're leaving. Why not tell Wyatt yourself?" Even as he spoke the words, he felt the answer deep down.

"You and I are more alike than you realize, son. I was pleased to see you kept the red suit. It fit pretty good with a little padding. Wear it in good health. It's helped a lot of children believe again."

Something foreign jarred loose in Rein. Believing.

"You realize, of course, how weird this is to be talking to an owl?"

"How do you think I feel?" his uncle answered.

"So, there is some truth to the legend that a spirit that was good on earth connects to an animal's spirit and lives on?"

"So it would seem. Damn glad it wasn't a grizzly. I wouldn't have been able to get very close before one of you took a pot shot at me."

"I miss you, Jed. We all do." For whatever reason, when he

didn't think too hard about it, talking to Jed the owl wasn't half bad.

"I miss you boys, too. But the ranch is in capable hands, the town is improving, and your families are growing."

"In case you hadn't noticed--"

"Believe, Rein. You see a table from a slab of wood, a frame from an old barn siding. Most folks don't put that much stock into believing in something. It's those that do that generally wind up reaping the reward."

"Sounds great, Uncle Jed, on a Hallmark card. I'm not sure how it applies in my case."

"Patience, boy, and determination."

The owl took flight and Rein leaned over the sink to watch it soar into the woods. The confusion he felt gave way to satisfaction. He grinned. His Uncle Jed had paid him a visit. Considering Dalton's cautionary words, he wasn't sure yet if this was good or bad.

Feeling as though he wasn't carrying quite as much weight on his shoulders, he slipped into bed a few moments later and snuggled close to Liberty.

She woke and pulled his arm around her, tucking it beneath her breast.

He nuzzled the soft spot just below her ear, pleased when she responded with her familiar sigh. She sat up and, without a word, drew her gown over her head and settled back in his arms.

The kiss they shared was slow and thorough. He savored the shape of her mouth, the taste of her lips, the satin-smooth skin beneath his fingertips. He knew her every curve, could navigate her body blind, knowing where she was ticklish, where to touch to get a sigh. And tonight it was all about the sighs.

Their love-making was unhurried. Desire simmered. The need to touch and be touched was what they both needed tonight. And when she opened her arms and he sank deep into her, he truly believed. "I am one lucky man."

She held his gaze, her body meeting his thrust for thrust. "I love you, Rein," she said, pulling his face to hers in a searing kiss as together they toppled into oblivion.

Chapter Five

"I THINK THAT'S IT." LIBERTY HANDED the itemized list of what was in each wrapped present to Ellie. It was more than enough for any child, and to some perhaps too much. "I admit going a little overboard," she told the woman. "But if I saw something that I thought Cody needed, or would like, I didn't show much restraint. Maybe you could hand some of them out to the other families at the house?"

Ellie smiled and shook her head. "This is very generous of you. I'm certain you could return some of these, if you still have the receipts."

Liberty shrugged. "I know you operate on a shoestring, especially at the holidays. Please use them as you see fit."

Ellie pondered the offer and then nodded. "Okay, thank you." She eyed Liberty. "I do have a favor I wanted to ask... well, actually, it's a favor from Rein."

She was driving over to the ranch to meet him as soon as she dropped off a meatloaf and mashed potato dinner at the Saunders' household. She had to make a quick stop at the bakery to pick up some honey clover leaf rolls first. "I'm heading over to see him at the ranch. Is there something you'd like me to pass along?"

She seemed hesitant, and then finally tossed her hands in the air. "I was hoping maybe I could convince him to play Kris Kringle for the kids at our family holiday party this coming Thursday."

The question took Liberty aback. "I can ask, but I can't guarantee how he'd feel about it. More importantly, how would Rowena feel about it?"

Ellie shrugged. "I'd say that we've asked one of our best donors to help us out. She's not going to want to spoil Christmas for Cody."

"How's he doing?" Liberty asked.

"Well, we've implemented an early start program for the little ones. It teaches reading, colors, alphabet, and a bit of writing. But he seems to be adapting well to the other children at the house."

Liberty nodded. "That's wonderful news."

"He still has his moments when he backs away from the other kids. We've noticed he's not as social when his mother is present as when she's gone."

"And Rowena, how's she doing?"

Ellie sighed. "I won't lie. It hasn't been easy. But to be fair, I think she is trying."

"Let me ask Rein, and I'll have him contact you," Liberty said. "I've got to run, but thank you for being Santa's helper." She started toward the bakery and stopped as she remembered something in her purse. "Would you see that Cody gets this sing-along video? It was one of his favorites."

Ellie took it and hugged Liberty. "That's what he's been asking for. I didn't understand." She glanced up at the darkening sky. It was barely three o'clock on Monday afternoon. "Better get going."

It had started to snow steadily in the short time it took for her to make her purchases and reach Sally's and Clay's house. Located just a couple of blocks off the main street square, it stood on a corner lot. In the spring, with its Victorian gabled roof and gingerbread trim, it was a postcard from the past. In winter, decorated with old-fashioned elegance, it was breathtaking. Sally had spent the better part of the last year renovating parts of her childhood home. A few years after her father's passing, she decided to place her stamp on the grand old house with her brand of Americana décor. It was during the renovation that she and Clay's relationship changed, turning into a whirlwind romance that led not only to marriage, but to the two of them now expecting twins.

She knocked on the back door. Peering through the window, she saw the lights on in the kitchen, but there was no sign of Sally. She checked the door and found it unlocked. "Sally?" She stuck her head inside and looked around. The new, open-concept family room at the back of the house flowed through the galley- style kitchen to the parlor-turned-music-room at the front of the house.

Liberty set the supper trays she'd carried in on the kitchen counter and peeked in the music room. It, too, was dark. Unusual, since Sally loved to put in a fire on chilly winter afternoons. "Sally?" She eyed the stairs and started up slowly, not wishing to startle her if she were lying down for a nap.

"I brought supper by for you and Clay." She peeked in the bathroom and then the bedroom. The woman couldn't have gotten far--she could barely waddle with the bundle she carried.

She heard a sound from the nursery and found Sally slumped in the rocking chair. She looked up—her face pale, eyes barely able to focus. She appeared delirious.

"Sally? Sweetheart, what happened?" Liberty knelt down and found the carpet wet beneath her. There was blood tinting the new carpet. Snatching her cell phone, she called Rein and then an ambulance.

By the time Rein and Clay arrived, the EMT's were loading Sally in the back of the ambulance, preparing to take her to Billings. Clay climbed inside, and Rein and Liberty followed in the truck.

"Dammit," Rein muttered as he followed the ambulance in the snowy weather. "She's too early."

Liberty clutched the door handle, eyeing the road. "The EMTs thought maybe it's preeclampsia. She may need a C-section." She looked at Rein, whose jaw was set firm as he drove. She reached out to touch his arm. "Honey, slow down. Clay's with her. She's going to the best hospital in the state."

Rein grabbed her hand and squeezed, and while he spoke no words she knew his thoughts were with hers, remembering the day he'd rushed her to Billings where they'd lost their son.

What seemed like hours later, they sat in the maternity waiting room at Billings Hospital. Dalton and Angelique had arrived, as had Aimee and Wyatt. The children were at the ranch under the watchful eyes of the Greyfeathers.

Sally had been wheeled in, seen quickly, and rushed to surgery, Clay close behind. The ambulance crew had been correct. Sally was close to being toxemic, which did not bode well for her or the twins.

Liberty held tightly to Rein's hand as they sat side-by-side. He hadn't said much on the drive, nor since their arrival. "Hey, do you want some coffee?" she asked.

He glanced up from his thoughts. "I'm good. You need anything?"

"Only for you to be okay," she said quietly.

He searched her eyes and she saw when he conceded to her request. "I know. I'm sorry. There's just been so much—" He held her gaze. "Just could use some good news, I guess."

Liberty nodded. "Not sure if this is the best time, but something different to think about. When I was talking to Ellie today, she asked if maybe you'd be interested in coming down on Thursday night this week to be Santa for the family holiday party at the house."

His wary expression spoke volumes. "What do you think of that idea?"

She shrugged. "I know it'd be hard seeing Cody, but then, at least one of us would get to see him open his barn."

Rein nodded.

At that moment, a flurry of doctors and nurses pushed through the doors of the surgical department.

Rein was on his feet, moving toward the doors, searching for someone to ask about what was going on. Clay exited the surgery area, his face drawn. Liberty had never before seen the man look afraid. Rein walked toward him and clamped his hand on the big man's shoulder. "Clay?"

Clay blinked. "One of the girls isn't doing well. She's having trouble getting oxygen. They may have to do surgery. They won't know until the pediatric surgeon can take a look at her x-rays."

"And Sally?" Rein asked.

Clay swiped his hand over his mouth. "She's doing okay. Holding her own. The other girl is hanging in there."

An entourage of friends stood around the two men. Liberty watched as Rein breathed a sigh of relief. "What do you need us to do for you?"

Clay looked at them. "Wait… and pray." He turned to head back through the swinging doors, back to his family.

Rein's concern for Sally was to be expected. After all, they'd dated at one time, and though Aimee had told her once that nothing had come of it, there would naturally be concern. Still, it accentuated the fact that she had not yet been able to give Rein the family he so desperately wanted. She left him sitting in the waiting room and wandered down the hall to the small cafeteria. Getting herself a cup of fresh coffee, she sat in a booth near one of the windows and stared at the snowfall in the lights of the parking lot.

"Hey, need some company?" Dalton stood at the table. He had a soda can in his hand.

Liberty nodded. "Have a seat." She glanced at him. "Everything okay?"

He lifted a brow. "That's what I came to ask you."

"What do you mean?"

"Come on, Liberty. I know this is hard on the both of you."

"Harder, I think, on Rein," she replied and averted her gaze.

"This isn't about losing your baby, is it?" Dalton asked.

Liberty fought her wayward emotions. Christmas had never been a stellar time for her anyway--at least, not until she'd met Rein. But before her, he'd dated Sally. And she couldn't shake the thought that he might wish it was him in that maternity room right now, instead of Clay.

"Hey, what's going on in that head of yours?" He tapped her shoulder with his soda can, forcing her gaze to his.

"Do you think, maybe…."

"Not for a minute." Dalton shook his head. "I had a feeling Rein's concern might be giving you doubts."

She swallowed. Her relationship with Rein before they began their summer fling had been nothing short of volatile. In fact, she'd deduced finally that the animosity between them had been a thinly wrapped veil of pent-up attraction that neither wanted to admit to. Once that line was crossed, sparks flew.

"Maybe we moved too fast. It was too soon after the fire. I was feeling so much guilt, I'd have said yes to anything he asked me."

Dalton narrowed his gaze. "And did you? Did you tell him yes, that you'd marry him, out of guilt, Liberty? Really? Because from where I stood, it looked like you won the lottery and Rein looked the same." He chuckled. "That day in Vegas, after you testified against your bozo ex-boss, when Rein got down on one knee on the courthouse steps and proposed…hell, I've never seen a man so smitten in my life—exception being me, of course."

His observation made her smile. "You and Angelique belong together. You have a beautiful family."

He eyed her. "Listen, Rein loves you. God knows what you see in the guy," he said with a smile. "But I know this as well as I know that I'm breathing."

She took her brother's hand and squeezed it. "It's just that he's experienced so much loss in his life. I wish I could give him what he wants."

A shadow fell over the table. "I wondered where you'd gone."

Dalton rose and patted Rein on the shoulder as he offered him his seat. "I'm going to text Betty. Figure that woman has a direct line to the big man upstairs."

Rein nodded, then edged in next to Liberty. "I caught just the last part of your conversation. Baby, what are you worried about?" he asked, shifting toward her and draping his arm over the booth behind her.

"There's just a lot going on right now. I know all you've been through and I wish…" Tears welled and she blinked them away.

He pulled her close. "Hey, we talked about this. And I meant what I said. I'm concerned for both Sally and Clay. I want things to go well for them just as we all do. But Liberty, as much as I'd like to have a family, it doesn't compare to how much I love you and want you by my side. Don't you ever forget that."

She buried her face in his shoulder, inhaling his all-male scent.

"Are you okay? Are we on the same page here?" he asked.

She nodded. "I'm sorry. I just know how much you wish

it was us having a child."

He hugged her tight. "And if that's what's supposed to be, then it will happen for us one day. Meantime, we can have fun trying, right?"

"Wild Thing" began to ring on his phone, and he pulled it out with a surprised look.

Liberty fished her phone from her jeans pocket. "Sorry, I think I might've butt-dialed you."

Rein glanced around at the empty cafeteria. "I love it when you talk dirty," he said with a grin.

She smacked his shoulder. "Seriously?"

"Hey, I'm sure there is a broom closet or something around here."

She shook her head. "Let me out and let's get back to the waiting room."

He lowered his head and kissed her softly. "You're sure?"

"I have to pee. Now move."

"I'll head back to the waiting room, then."

Liberty walked across the hall to the restroom. She splashed her face with cold water and, taking a deep cleansing breath, caught a whiff of the potent hospital disinfectant used when cleaning. Her stomach lurched and she ran to the stall just in time.

∞

Rein glanced up from where he stood with Dalton as they waited for the surgical auxiliary lady to make a fresh pot of coffee. She was a spry, gray-haired woman with bright blue eyes and a gentle smile. Completing her mission, she offered magazines to another family waiting across the hall, then settled back at her desk to resume her knitting.

Betty arrived close to ten, after she'd closed the café and gotten Jerry tucked in at home. She'd gathered them together at one end of the room, insisting they hold hands and pray for Sally, Clay, and their family. After a few minutes, Dalton slipped away to get a cup of coffee. Rein followed him.

"You and Liberty get things straightened out?" Dalton asked, filling up his Styrofoam cup.

Rein glanced at his brother. "Yeah, we did."

Dalton smiled. "That's good. You guys still trying, I presume?"

Rein chuckled. "Is this any of your business?"

"Hey, dude. She opened up to me. And she is my half-sister. So, yeah, maybe a little," Dalton answered. "Besides, I care about the both of you."

"Aw, that's sweet," Rein said with a grin.

"Asshat," Dalton muttered.

"By the way, had a visit the other night."

Dalton's gaze darted to his. "Really?"

"Yep, thought I was going looney-toons."

Dalton nodded. "Sounds about right."

"Don't you want to know what he said?"

"Okay, sure." Dalton leaned against the hospitality counter.

"He's happy with what we've done with the ranch, for starters. Happy to see Michael involved, but we shouldn't work him too hard."

Dalton tipped his head and stared at Rein. "Are you making this up?"

Rein held up his hand. "God's truth, unless I was under the influence of Jamison."

Dalton raised his brows. "Anything else?"

There was more, but Rein preferred to keep the rest between him and Jed—at least, for now. "Not really."

Dalton shook his head. "I thought when it happened to me that I was crazy." He looked at Rein. "But I guess we all can't be crazy… right?"

Rein lifted his mouth in a half grin and gave his brother a dubious look.

Dalton used his cup to hide his finger, flipping off Rein.

The surgery door swung open and Clay walked out cradling a small bundle in his arms. The wide grin on his face masked the fact that he'd neither slept nor shaved in several hours. His countenance fell when the pediatric surgeon followed from the surgery area.

"Mr. Saunders?" the man asked, approaching Clay.

Clay lifted his chin, appearing to steel himself for what news might follow. "That's me. Is this about my daughter?"

Rein reached for Liberty's hand as the small crowd stood to offer Clay support. She'd returned from the cafeteria a few minutes after him, looking green around the gills. Waving it off as being tired and stressed, she'd joined the others in their prayer vigil.

The man placed his hand on Clay's shoulder. "First, your daughter's going to be just fine."

Clay dropped his head back and squeezed his eyes shut before facing the doctor. "Oh, man, thank you. Thank you."

"She had what we call TTN, or Transient Tachypnea of the Newborn. Basically, fluid got into her lungs, making her have to breathe harder. It's fairly rare in preemies, but sometimes happens in Cesarean deliveries simply because the fluid isn't squeezed out like it would be during a vaginal birth."

"Is she going to be okay? Will this affect her as she grows?" Clay asked.

"Not usually. We've got her on a breathing machine now, just until the fluids clear out and she can breathe on her own. I expect she'll be ready to go home with her family in two or three days. When your wife gets settled in her room, I'll see that you both get up to see your daughter."

"Aubrey," Clay said. "Her name is Aubrey."

The doctor, who appeared to be in his mid-to-late thirties, smiled. "I'll let the nurses know." He leaned over and pulled back the blanket to take a peek at the newborn in Clay's arms. "Both girls?"

"Yessir," Clay said with pride marking his response. "This is Ava."

The doctor chuckled. "I have twin girls of my own in middle school right now. Please accept my condolences." He patted Clay on the back and gave him a grin.

"Gavin Beauregard, is that you?" Betty skirted around the crowd and held her arms out to the surprised man. "I haven't seen you since you were knee-high to a grasshopper. How's your mama?"

The doctor peered at Betty with a frown. "I'm sorry, ma'am. Do I know you?" He smiled and took her hands in his.

Dalton raised his brows and glanced at Rein, as if to say, "this woman knows no strangers."

"Back in the day, before Jerry swept me north, I lived in New Orleans. I remember your mama when she'd come into my daddy's market to buy his special Cajun seasoning."

"Did either of you know that?" Wyatt whispered as he came up behind his brothers.

Rein looked from one to the other. "I've never heard her mention it. But that might explain the café serving grits twenty-four seven."

The physician narrowed his gaze. "You're not that Betty?" His face brightened. "I remember now. I must have been what? Six, maybe seven at the time?" He shook his head. "What a small world." He chuckled. "My mama is doing fine. Still likes to cook Cajun cuisine, but daddy doesn't fancy it much. His tastes run a little bland for a New Orleans resident." He winked at Betty. "I do miss my mama's cooking."

Betty pulled him into an unexpected bear hug. "Well, now, we have no strangers in this bunch. You'll have to come up to End of the Line sometime to try some of my cooking. I might even whip up some shrimp and grits, if I can find any worthy around here." She smiled and patted his hand.

He rolled his eyes heavenward in appreciation of the offer. "I may just take you up on that, Miss Betty."

He slapped Clay on the shoulder. "Congratulations, but if you'll excuse me. I've got a patient... uh, Miss Aubrey to check on and some paperwork to catch up on." He looked at Clay. "We'll be in touch a little later."

Clay shook the doctor's hand. "Thank you."

Ava Marie Saunders spent the next few moments being the rock star of the enamored audience of the Billings maternity ward waiting room.

Rein sat down next to Liberty as she held the sleeping child. Life was damn funny, he thought. Once, his whole life was about cattle and wondering about his next construction contract. Now, he dreamt of moments like this. "Hey, you hold that baby like a pro."

"You want to hold her?"

Rein eyed the tiny package. She appeared far too small, too delicate for his big, rough hands. Without thought, he rubbed his hands nervously over his knees. "Yeah... she's little, really little." He glanced up and met Liberty's beautiful gaze.

"You won't break her."

"I might," he said, offering a wry smile. Her tiny head alone would fit in the palm of his hand.

She handed him the child, and Rein's heart faltered at the enormous sense of responsibility that washed over him.

"Just cradle her in the crook of your arm," Liberty guided him. "There, just make sure you have her head supported."

She leaned back and smiled. "Just like a pro."

He'd held his niece, Gracie, and his little nephew, Sawyer, only a few months old, but neither seemed as fragile as tiny Ava. Once tucked in his arms, however, he couldn't take his eyes off her, nor could he stop thinking about Cody and how being called dad had affected him.

Thursday morning, Rein woke to the sound of Liberty in the bathroom. He walked in, carefully pushing open the door, and found her on her knees, viciously scrubbing the tub. He blinked a couple of times, and checked the clock on the bedside table over his shoulder. It took a couple of blinks to register that it read five a.m. "Honey, are we expecting guests?"

Her dark hair was drawn up in a ponytail and she was wearing her cotton pajama bottoms and a T-shirt. Given the sweet dream he'd been having; he was more than ready to haul her back to bed—pink Playtex gloves included.

She glanced up at him as she blew a wisp of hair from her face. "This tub was a mess." She returned to her task with renewed fervor.

Rein stared at her fine little ass bouncing gingerly with her intensity. The cotton knit fabric molded every curve. He knelt down beside her. "You need some help?" He eyed the narrow swath of bare skin showing between her shirt and waistband. "This kind of thing can be hard on your back, sweetheart."

He rubbed his hand over her back, dipping between her thighs.

She shot him a look. "You know I'm trying to work here." Her sentence hitched when he stroked her once.

"So am I. What's a guy to do when he wakes up to his

wife's ass—mind you, exquisite ass—flashing him in the face?"

"Me cleaning turns you on?" She leaned on her elbows, her hips pushing back against his fingers.

"Sweetheart," he whispered against her temple. "Everything about you turns me on."

She drew up on her knees to face him, tossing the gloves into the sink. She cradled his face in her hands and captured his mouth in a no-nonsense kiss. "You need a shower," she said.

He pulled her to her feet and stepped in the shower, drawing her in after him. "I need more than a shower, darlin'."

An hour later, they sat together at the kitchen island. Liberty nursed a cup of tea and poked at a bowl of oatmeal that she thought had sounded good until placed in front of her.

Rein reached out, taking her hand. "Sweetheart, are you feeling okay? Maybe you should make an appointment to see Doc Johnson."

She squeezed his hand. "I'm fine. I just haven't slept well, thinking about everything."

"Hey, you sure I should go down to Billings tonight? I can ask Wyatt or Dalton to step in as Kris Kringle." He studied her face. She looked pale.

"I'll be fine. Clay and Sally are coming home today and we've been planning some meals to take over until Julie gets back to help out. I have them in the freezer--I'd just planned to stop by a little later to drop them off."

"If you like, I can drop the food by on my way to Billings. It'd save you getting out in the cold." He eyed her. "Maybe you're coming down with something, sweetheart."

She dismissed his concern. "Rein, there's no need to baby me. I'm just tired. With Cody and the holiday gathering, and now Clay and Sally's twins born early—I just have a lot to accomplish before Christmas."

He smiled softly, tucking a stray shock of hair behind her ear. "Which is why you're cleaning the tub at the crack of dawn?"

"Cleaning relaxes me," she said, giving him a side-glance.

He took her hand, kissed the inside of her wrist, and smiled. "Here I always thought it was me. Looks like I'm going to have to step things up. You suppose that adult store outside Billings has a mop and maybe a bucket?"

She eyed him. "You are a sick man, you know that?"

"Yeah, but damn, girl, you married me, didn't you?" He gave her a wicked grin.

"That I did." She smiled and shook her head. Taking a few steps toward the sink, she paused a moment and seemed to be getting her balance when Rein noticed her knees begin to buckle.

He lunged for her, catching her before she fell, easing her to the floor. He realized she'd fainted, and when he got no response from her, he called the ambulance, now on speed-dial. Within the hour they were on their way to Billings for the second time that week.

Four hours later, Rein sat in a chair beside Liberty. Her face was pale against the sterile white hospital sheets. She'd come in severely dehydrated, and drifted in and out of consciousness the past few hours. They'd admitted her to run tests in order to determine why, exactly, she'd fainted other than being dehydrated. He wasn't about to leave her side, not even when Aimee offered to give him a break.

Sally and Clay had stopped in before heading back to End of the Line to take their girls home. Wyatt, who readily accepted taking over the Santa role at Miss Ellie's holiday party, also assisted in getting the prepared food down to the Saunders' house.

Sitting in the hospital, watching daylight turn to dusk and snow begin to fall, Rein thought about when the roles had been reversed. When he'd been shot, he fought to heal from his wounds because he didn't want to lose her. A myriad of possible concerns flitted through his mind. He couldn't lose her, too.

"Hey." Liberty opened her eyes. "How long have I been asleep?"

He scooted his chair closer to the bed and reached for her hand. "You've been drifting in and out for a few hours. Just in this past hour have you slept soundly."

She glanced outside. Her eyes darted suddenly to his. "What about the party? Ellie and the kids?"

He squeezed her hand. "It's all good, including the food you made for Clay and Sally. Wyatt and Aimee have it under control."

"I'm sorry. This is silly. I just haven't been taking very good care of myself."

Rein brought her hand to his lips, leaving a kiss on her fingers. "The nurse said that the doc should be around soon with an update on the tests they ran. God knows they took enough of your blood for a transfusion." Rein smiled. "You hungry?"

She looked up at him. Dark circles shadowed her beautiful eyes. "Not really, thanks. How about you, did you eat?"

"A nurse brought in your lunch, but you were sleeping. I helped myself to the pudding cup."

"Of course you did." She smiled, then glanced at the carafe on the nightstand. "Is there any water in there?" She licked her lips.

He poured a glass and helped as she took a few sips through the straw. "Better?"

She nodded and lay wearily back on her pillow. She shut her eyes.

"You want to sleep some more?" he asked.

She shook her head. By the expression on her face, he

saw that she was fighting with her emotions.

"Sweetheart," he said, brushing the hair from her forehead," it's going to be okay." He leaned down and kissed her softly.

"Rein, there's something I need to tell you." She took a deep breath.

"Honey, you can tell me anything." His gut twisted, even though he meant what he said.

"I didn't think it would matter. The doctors told me it wouldn't." She looked up at him. Tears seeped from the corners of her eyes. "I should have said something, early on."

Rein searched her face. "Baby, whatever it is won't make a difference in how much I love you."

She turned her face from him. "I hope you'll feel the same after I tell you."

He turned her face to meet his gaze. "Liberty, you know you can always tell me—"

"I had an abortion." She held his gaze.

Reins' heart seemed to drop in his chest.

"It was long before I met you." She averted her eyes directly from his. "I'm not proud of it. But I was young—too young to be pregnant—and I—" She struggled with the words. "I didn't want to be a mom back then." Tears flowed in rivulets down her temples. "They told me it'd be okay. That I should be able to have children again, but they warned me of the risk—the chance that I might not be able to due to complications."

She broke down then, great sobs shaking her shoulders. He held her hand, absorbing the information, not knowing what kind of doctor she'd seen, how experienced they were in such things. He blew out a long breath, looked away, and, rubbing his hand over his mouth, walked to the window. He stood a moment, staring at the snow-covered cars in the parking lot.

"Rein, I'm sorry I didn't say something sooner. But I've wanted to tell you from the moment we started talking about a family." Her face crumpled. "Now I'm afraid that what they told me back then wasn't true." Her voice cracked as she rambled on—verbally flogging herself for the choices she'd made in the past.

"Stop." He said, looking back at her. "Stop it, Liberty." He walked over and sat on the bed, pulling her into his arms. "You'll stop this now. Stop feeling guilty. Stop beating yourself up." He rocked her softly, all the while saying a silent prayer that those doctors had been good, reputable, and right. That she'd have no complications in being able to bear and carry a child. "It's going to be okay, sweetheart. Either way, we've got each other. We've got our family. It's going to be—"

"Mr. Mackenzie?" Dr. Stephens, one of the family practice physicians associated with the Billings hospital, stood inside the door. In his hand was a clipboard with several papers attached to it.

Rein stood. Holding Liberty's hand in his, he faced the white-haired man. His cell phone jangled in his pocket, but he ignored it. Finally, he apologized and looked at the caller I.D. "It's Ellie. Should I take it?" It was long past time when the party should have started. He'd gotten a text earlier from Wyatt saying the suit still fit. The ringing stopped, and he tucked the phone in his pocket. "I'm sorry. Please continue." But he couldn't shake the weird feeling in his gut.

"Well, after running a number of tests—"

Rein's phone rang again. Once more, it was Ellie's number.

At that moment, the doctor's pager went off and he read the code. "I'm sorry, folks, this will have to wait. It seems we have an emergency situation coming in."

Rein answered his phone. "Ellie? What's up?"

"Rein, there's been a shooting," she began.

"What? A shooting? Wyatt. Is Wyatt okay?" His heart began to race.

"He managed to get most of the kids into the back room with me and one of the other staff members."

"Ellie! Is Wyatt okay?" Rein knuckles were turning white.

"I think so. The medics are bringing him to Billings Hospital. They should almost be there."

Cody. Rein closed his eyes and took a deep breath. "The kids—Cody—is everyone okay?" Rein fought past the lump in his throat. God, please don't take Cody away from me.

"He's fine. Frightened, but okay, I think. I'm afraid that it had to do with Rowena. The two came in looking for her. They started shooting." There was a pause. "They aren't sure she'll make it. I'm with Cody. He keeps asking for his daddy."

Rein's hand flew to his heart. Never again would he doubt Emilee's gift.

"The police insist that everyone be checked out. They killed the two men before they could shoot anyone else. Rowena knew them. She tried to stop them."

"Jesus," Rein said in way of prayer as he paced the floor, listening. "I'll see you when you get here."

"How's Liberty? Wyatt told me why he was filling in."

His gaze met Liberty's. "We're going to be fine." It felt more like a decree than a prayer. "See you soon."

He sat on the edge of the bed. "They're bringing in Rowena and Wyatt."

She clutched his hand. "Are they okay? Ellie and Cody, everyone?"

He nodded. "She thinks so. But the police suggested they all come up and be checked."

"And the people who did this?" she asked.

"Ellie said the police shot two men who'd come in demanding to see Rowena."

"Payback," Liberty said. "Trust me, my father was the king of payback."

"Because of her plea bargaining, giving up those names." He shook his head. "Baby, I need to go check on Wyatt and Cody, okay?"

"Of course, go. I'm fine. Really."

"You're sure?"

"Go," she said, "and be sure to call Aimee."

Epilogue

IT WAS A CHRISTMAS EVE to remember at the Kinnison ranch this year. Amid the flurry of news of the new twins in town, and the tragedy striking Miss Ellie's shelter, a surge of community camaraderie spread like wildfire, along with word-of-mouth invitations to the Kinnison holiday gathering. From noon on, a steady stream of friends, family, and townsfolk had been filtering in and out, bringing greetings, food, and non-perishable items to donate to Miss Ellie's shelter pantry.

Wyatt, his leg in a cast from where a bullet whizzed through his calf, miraculously missing bone, sat in a chair reading and re-reading Jed's traditional Christmas story to any kid (or adult) who wanted to hear it. Sadie slept on the floor beside him, oblivious to the chaos disrupting her household.

Clay and Sally had decided that this was a not-to-be missed event for their week-old twin daughters—Ava and Aubrey. The family held court in one corner of the massive living room where they received advice and well-wishes— not to mention baby-sitting offers from several folks who'd stopped by.

Liberty sat on the couch watching Rein carry in more wood for the fire. Outside, Michael Greyfeather and Dalton offered short sleigh rides across the snowy back pasture after Emilee decided to come in and play with her cousins.

Her eyes bright with the spirit of Christmas, Emilee

plopped down on the couch next to Liberty. "How are you, Aunt Liberty?"

Liberty smiled at the young girl and took her hand to give it a squeeze. "Just fine, Miss Emilee, and ready to open up a can on you in a game of checkers whenever you're ready."

Emilee didn't respond right away, but stared at their entwined hands.

"Em?" Liberty eyed the girl as she nudged her.

She looked up at Liberty, her eyes wide with delight.

"Don't. Say. A. Word." Liberty leaned down nose-to-nose with the girl.

Liberty looked up when Ellie came through the front door. Cody stood at her side, his face drawn. Liberty wondered if they were strong enough to help him through the horror of his mother's death. If love would be enough to instill the sense of security lost to such a tragedy.

Cody's gaze quickly scanned the roomful of people until he found Rein, who had just risen from tending the fireplace. "Dad," he yelled and ran across the room, leaping into Rein's outstretched arms. He buried his face in Rein's shoulder as he hugged his neck.

Swallowing the lump in her throat, Liberty swiped the tears from her cheeks and walked to meet the two. She brushed her hand over Cody's angel fine hair.

Ellie joined them. "Here's his backpack," she told Liberty, then motioned her aside to speak privately. "The judge accepted Mrs. Conner's recommendation that Cody be placed in temporary custody with the two of you."

"Oh, that's wonderful news. Isn't that the woman from Social Services who stopped by our house that day?"

Ellie smiled. "Yes, and apparently she was quite impressed with you both. She gave the judge her report from that day. It should go a long way in helping the judge to decide on permanent custody."

"And Rowena? There's no other family?" Liberty asked.

"None that has shown up thus far." She shrugged. "The aunt up north she spoke of wasn't real. It's very sad. I wish I could have done more to help her."

Liberty took Ellie's hand. "You did the best you could, Ellie. You always do. No one could have predicted this would happen."

"I know, but it doesn't make it any easier." Her smile didn't reach her eyes.

Liberty watched Rein speaking quietly to the child. "Cody's going to need some special help, I think, to get over this. What a horrific thing to experience."

"For an adult or child." She glanced at Cody, who had a death grip around Rein's neck. "We've arranged for counselors to come in and speak with everyone at the house. And we're revisiting our security policies. We just can't have this happen again." She looked at Liberty and squeezed her hand. "But today is Christmas Eve, and I think we should enjoy and be thankful for those around us." She glanced toward Angelique and the baby she held. "If I'm lucky, I'll get to hold Sawyer a few minutes before his daddy comes back. It's tough prying that little one away from Dalton."

"Agreed," Liberty said, and pulled the woman into a warm hug. "Merry Christmas, Ellie."

"Merry Christmas, Liberty, and thank you, both, for all you've done."

Liberty's phone buzzed in her back pocket. She peeked at the number. It was a call she'd been waiting for. Turning to face the cathedral windows, she looked out on the blanket of fresh snow. In the distance, she saw Michael Greyfeather bringing the sleigh across the field. "Hello, Dr. Stephens. Merry Christmas, and thank you for taking such good care of my brother, Wyatt in the ER the other night. We all appreciate what you did." She paused taking a fortifying breath. "About my tests. Do you have some news for me?"

"I do," he said. "And provided you abide by a few staunch rules, young lady, I think you're going to be able to carry this one to term."

She bit her lip to keep from squealing. "You're sure?"

"As sure as I can be, Liberty. Things can and do happen. I don't need to tell you that. But based on the fact that you're already almost to your second trimester, I'd say things are looking very good."

"Thank you, Dr. Stephens. This is a wonderful Christmas gift for both Rein and me."

"Don't thank me just yet, Liberty. I want to put you on a strict regimen of plenty of water, rest, and getting enough protein in your diet. If you don't, I'll have to sic my nurses on you, and trust me, they make a New York fishwife seem docile."

She smiled. "I understand."

A movement outside caught her eye, and a snowy owl landed on the corner of the deck railing. Its great yellow eyes blinked at her. She grinned and placed her hand on the cool glass, watching as the great bird flew off into the tall pine forest.

She sniffed and turned to find Rein. Their gazes met across the room. He pointed at Cody and sat him on the ottoman beside Emilee. He tossed her a wink as Emilee looked over her shoulder and placed her arm around Cody, tucking him in as they waited for Wyatt to read the story. Rein skirted around the edge of the room, ducking into the one of the bedrooms down the hall to transform into Santa with the help of Jed's suit. She swallowed the lump that had formed suddenly in her throat. There was so much to be grateful for.

Though the week had been riddled with sorrow—three

lives lost in senseless violence, a young boy orphaned, the lives of others changed forever—somehow, someway, the world righted itself again. Love found a way through the worst of situations. "I'm fine, Dr. Stephens. Truly, I have all I want for Christmas… and so much more."

"That's true for all of us. On that note, I will bid you Merry Christmas and see the both of you next Tuesday," he said.

"We'll be there."

Sometime later, after the guests had gone and the remaining family had been bedded down for the night awaiting Christmas morning, Liberty stood with Rein in his old room as he prepared to retire the suit for another year. "Santa, have you got a minute? I didn't get to tell you what I wanted for Christmas."

He grinned and pulled her onto his lap as he sat in the overstuffed reading chair he'd made. She wrapped her arms around his neck.

"Well, now Miss Liberty Belle," Rein said in his best Santa voice. "Have you been a good little girl this year?"

She leaned down and whispered in his ear. "You know I have, Santa."

Affirmation flickered in Rein's blue eyes. He cleared his throat. "And what would you like for Christmas?" he asked, his gaze holding hers.

"All I want for Christmas this year is my husband, and our lovely boy, Cody." She paused as if in thought. "Oh, and a newly designed nursery where my husband's office used to be."

He pulled off the fake beard, wrapped his hand around the back of her neck, and drew her into a soft, thorough kiss. "Already thinking of some ideas." He grinned, searching her eyes as she backed away.

Liberty eyed him, realizing then that her secret had been

revealed. "She told you."

Rein kissed her again. "About ten seconds after you left the couch to talk with Ellie." He pulled her into his arms. "Don't be upset, sweetheart. Everyone already knows. I'm pretty sure Aimee's already planning a shower."

"Seriously, can't there be any surprises in this family?" Liberty stood, planting her hands on her hips.

Rein grinned and held out his hand. "Hey, you want a surprise?"

She eyed him warily. "Should I lock the door?"

He stood. "Probably."

He pulled out his cell phone and, after a moment, laid it on the nightstand. He guided Liberty to the edge of the bed and stood in front of her. The music began, and Liberty recognized the chords of Mariah Carey's rendition of one of her favorite songs, "All I Want for Christmas."

"I don't need a lot this Christmas," Rein crooned as he began to remove the Santa suit.

Liberty shook her head and tried not to laugh. So some of the words were questionable. The intent was right. Apparently, surprises were still alive and well in End of the Line. "Is that a candy cane in your pocket, or are you just glad to see me?" she asked with a wry grin.

"But there is something I need." Clearly on a roll, he pulled the Velcro closure open with one yank and tossed the coat aside, revealing suspenders over his sleeveless muscle shirt.

"Are you seriously stripping for me?" she asked, tugging at one of the suspenders.

He offered a wicked grin. "Turnabout is fair play," he said, referring to a time when he'd asked the same from her during their torrid summer affair. "You wanted a surprise. I aim to give the lady what she wants." He danced and offered some seriously tantalizing moves through to the next chorus—piece by piece, leaving all notions of Santa on the floor. "All I want for Christmas," he sang, turning to face her without a stitch, and pointed at her with more than just his fingers.

She raised her brow. "Hell, yeah, you can surprise me anytime, cowboy."

And he did. More than once.

Dear Reader,

I loved revisiting End of the line, especially at my favorite time of the year—Christmas! There is so much community spirit, traditions that remind me of my own small-town upbringing, which I am able now to appreciate so much more than I did when I was young. There's more on the horizon for the folks in End of the Line, Montana—new visitors, new generations, and with it new businesses. In celebration of Betty's new bakery, Sunrise Bakery—I'd like to share one of the special recipes for Christmas that is tradition around our house. These are great for tucking into a tin or gift box and giving out as special gifts during the holiday. (Provided they make it out of the house!)

Watch for more recipes coming from Betty's Café and the Sunrise Bakery!

CRACKLY GINGER COOKIES

2 cp. sifted flour ★ *2 tsp. baking soda* ★ *1 tsp. cinnamon* ★ *1 tsp ginger* ★ *½ tsp cloves*
1 tsp salt ★ *¾ cp. oleo or butter (softened)* ★ *1 cp. white sugar* ★ *1 egg* ★ *¼ cp. dark molasses.*

Sift dry ingredients. Cream butter and sugar. Add egg and molasses. Beat with mixer until fluffy. Stir in dry ingredients. Chill (30-40 min) Roll into walnut size balls. Roll in sugar. Bake on greased baking sheet 350 oven for 10 minutes.

Read more about Rein and Liberty's tumultuous beginnings in the Kinnison Legacy trilogy.

Here is a sneak peek to

RUSTLER'S HEART!

Enjoy!

RUSTLERS HEART

(Book II, Kinnison Legacy)

Chapter One

REIN WIPED THE SAWDUST ON his jeans, grabbed his coffee mug, and took a long swallow. He'd been up since before dawn, starting in on the details left to make the cabin ready by Friday.

Since Aimee's arrival at the ranch on a semi-permanent basis, he'd spent more time on the cabins for more reasons than simply giving them privacy. Wyatt had had a sudden change in heart about the project. He'd relinquished hold on his share of the ranch in order to collectively refinance and put more money into permits and materials to build the cabins and ready them for use. They'd given themselves a target date of two years to complete the project. Dalton, Michael Greyfeather and Tyler Janzen from Janzen Plumbing and Heating had come on board to help. That gave Rein the freedom to do what he loved which was to design and build the rustic furniture that would grace the interior of each cabin.

However, Wyatt's unexpected news recently of a woman named Liberty who claimed to be their half-sister, punched up the clock for completion of the sample cabin when she stated she needed a place to stay. The idea of having a half-sister hadn't settled well with Dalton, and frankly Rein questioned why she would suddenly make contact after all of this time. Then again, she was only twenty-one, a kid in most respects, still fishing around to find her place in this world.

He stood for a moment at the screen door to the back-yard and assessed whether there would be time to put in the brick patio he'd planned. The crisp spring air invigo-rated him. He loved to wake early and watch the sun climb high in the sky as it burned off the heavy mist over the mountains. Last night he lay awake on the cot he'd brought down to the cabin and with the windows open, listened to the sounds of the creek and the forest that had become a part of him. He'd come to the ranch a grieving young man, bitter about the way things had turned out for him, but found serenity and purpose in the ability to use his hands to create something from natures bountiful resources. His Uncle Jed had taught him to give back to the land and to others. For him, it was the force that drove his inspiration to see his uncle's dream become a reality.

"I see you couldn't sleep, either." Dalton rubbed his eyes and let the screen door slam behind him.

Rein had just finished shaving down the front door pre-pared to place it in the frame when he had more help. Dalton spotted the cot set up in the corner of the living room and made a beeline for the coffee maker on the kitchen counter. "All the comforts of home. You may have a roommate soon if those two can't keep it down."

"You're just in time. Grab those hinges and help me get this up." He lifted the solid pine door from the sawhorses set up in the middle of the vacant cabin. He was glad he'd cho-sen to put in a tile floor with the heat conductors beneath. With the three of them hard at work yesterday, they'd man-aged to accomplish getting the bedrooms, bath, and kitchen ready. Now they only needed Tyler to come in and do his thing with the plumbing. Aimee offered to pick up a few necessities to complete a temporary living arrangement—a few dishes, pots and pans, toaster and other incidentals that she would pick up when she went in to Billings this week for the last fitting of her wedding dress.

Rein slipped the shims into place and had Dalton hold the door steady while he drilled in the hinges. "You do look a bit haggard this morning, Dal." Rein smiled.

Dalton narrowed his bloodshot eyes on him. "We're going to need to get another cabin ready. Those two are like rabbits... loud rabbits." He blew out a weary sigh.

Rein chuckled. Of course, he'd had a good night's sleep after he chose to come down to the cabin. He couldn't have been happier to see Wyatt rescued from the self-imposed prison he was in. Aimee had changed him and for the better, but at the same time it sent a ripple of change through all their lives. Dalton as a rule was less receptive to change. He liked continuity, liked for things to be a certain way—in particular, his way. Though Rein knew that Dalton wished nothing but happiness for his brother.

"I was so damn tired this morning from listening to those two last night that I nearly forgot the new rule of not walking naked through the house." He scrunched his face and rubbed a hand over his unshaven cheek. "Aimee just about caught me in my all together suit if it hadn't been for those throw things on the couch."

Rein shook his head and laughed. "Okay, let's see if this works." Dalton stepped back and Rein opened and shut the door several times to check for fit. He'd get around to adding a lock later. They'd never had any trouble with prowlers of the two-legged variety at the ranch--raccoons, snakes and the occasional curious skunk were the worst offenders.

Dalton trudged across the room to refill his cup.

"That about does it. Tyler said he'd be out later today." Rein flipped a switch and set in motion on an overhead light and fan combination in the middle of the living room ceiling. He studied it and was pleased to see that the balance was correct and the fan blades were nearly silent, even at high speed. He shut the light off and looked at Dalton. "I think we're ready to haul the furniture up from the workshop."

Dalton eyed him. "You really like this, don't you?" he asked.

He picked up the broom, swept up the mess of sawdust he'd created, and dumped it into a box of debris ready to burn. "Getting to watch you work your ass off? Nothing makes me happier." He tossed Dalton a grin and received the finger in return.

"I mean this whole thing—this project." Dalton waved his hand over the room.

Rein shrugged. After he graduated with his business/marketing degree, he returned to the ranch to help by using his expertise, but it was the discovery of his Uncle's private journal that outlined in specific detail his plans for the ranch that became his inspiration. Reading the journal, he saw himself between the pages and realized the idea was born of Jed's experience of raising three 'lost' boys without a home and no clue where their lives were headed. It was in taking on his Uncle's vision that Rein began to utilize a love he'd always had of design, and building with his hands. Eventually, it was Wyatt, who suggested that he turn the third section of the multi-car garage into a workshop.

Rein leaned against the counter and gestured to Dalton with his cup. There was no better smell in the world than fresh coffee and wood shavings. "I just love to build shit. You know that." He brushed off his comment and blew across his coffee.

"Yeah, it's more than that, isn't it?" Dalton prodded.

Rein sighed and shrugged his shoulder. "I don't know, maybe. I'm twenty-nine, I have no kids, no wife or even a prospect of one. I've spent most of my life on this ranch.

Maybe this is what I can create to leave as my legacy. Besides, from a business standpoint, if we can get this off the ground and rent out these cabins, we could put the ranch on the map, as well as improve things for End of the Line. More tourists equal more money, equals more business, equals…"

"Yeah, I got it." Dalton sipped his coffee and studied him. "And you think that's what Jed wanted?"

Rein shrugged. "His journal kind of intimates it, yeah. He was part of the chamber as you remember. He was always looking for new ideas to help, improve the community. You know that as well as me."

Dalton nodded. A short silence stretched between them.

Rein narrowed his gaze and studied the man who was as close as any blood brother. "You aren't normally this chatty of a morning. What's up? I have a feeling you're leading up to whatever is really bugging you. So let's get it out, because I haven't got all day to try to wrestle it out of you." He knew Dalton's moods like the back of his hand. Of the two brothers, he'd spent more time with Dalton, especially on business trips. Rein had the book knowledge for running the ranch, while Dalton was a good old boy with a flair for schmoozing the socks off the stingiest buyer. His only downfall was he drank too much. More than once, Rein and Wyatt had had to rescue Dalton from many a late night bar episode, and he realized that his troubled brother was still running from the demons in his past. Rein couldn't imagine what being abandoned by his mom would do to a kid, but he'd observed the results of in both men he considered older brothers. Wyatt, who'd tried once tried to regain a normal life with a woman he'd fallen in love with was burnt. They accepted his choice to be a recluse that is the persistent school teacher taught him a hard lesson about love. Things were good now and with their wedding around the corner, even better. But Dalton found solace for his past in a bottle and, so far, nothing had been able to pull him away from his rebellious ways. Rein considered himself lucky in some respects, his grief eventually gave way to the realization that for the time he had them on this earth, his parents cared about him, just as Jed had done. Maybe that's why he felt such a vested interest in seeing this project through. Rein took a wild stab at what his gut sensed was Daltons problem. "This is about Liberty, right?"

Dalton shrugged as though the topic alone was hard to handle. "I don't know. It just doesn't feel right. I mean what if this broad has some crazy vendetta, you know? I have no idea what kind of picture Eloise painted of me and Wyatt."

"Broad? You do realize you're talking about your half-sister, right? What are you saying... like she's going after you with a chainsaw in the middle of the night or something?" Rein laughed.

Dalton raised a brow.

"You've watched too many of those damn crime shows." He put his cup down and stretched out the kink in his back from sleeping on the cot. "I guess we'll find out a few days."

Dalton didn't respond and Rein felt compelled to convince him he was out of line with this. "From what Wyatt told us about her, it doesn't appear she's the serial killer type."

"That's just it. All he knows is what she told him. How do we know if any of it is true? How can we be certain of anyone's background that chooses to come here? That's my chief concern."

He considered Dalton's comments. "You make a valid point and like Wyatt said, that is something we're going to have to address when we begin drawing up the rental agreements. But really, there is a multitude of ways to do a background check on someone if a person wanted to."

Dalton shrugged. "Yeah, you're right. I should do one on

this Liberty chick. Good idea, bro." He reached over and slapped Rein on the shoulder.

He hated to feed into Dalton's obvious displeasure with Wyatt's decision to allow Liberty to come in and live off them until who knows when. But if there was one thing Rein despised more than anything, it was a freeloader and if little Miss Liberty thought for one minute that she was going to stay here, eat their food and use their services for free, she was in for a serious wakeup call.

Curious now, Rein rinsed out his cup and pulled on his work gloves. "Let me know what you find out. Meantime, let's head over and pick up that furniture before that storm blows in."

Dalton finished his cup and frowned as he followed him out the door. "In case you hadn't noticed, the sun is brilliant and there isn't a cloud in the sky."

Rein fished the keys to his truck out of his pocket and eyed the sky above. "Yeah, but I heard an owl outside the cabin last night."

Dalton rolled his eyes to the heavens. "Jeez, you and Wyatt and that damn American Indian mumbo-jumbo."

Rein just tossed him a smile.

She checked her watch. Ticket in hand, Liberty waited on the scarred wood bench at the seedy bus station in the worst possible area of town. The clerk, safe behind her bulletproof glass and steel barred office looked out with a sullen face at the handful of passengers who waited for the nine-thirty bus. She looked again at the schedule, with a couple of transfers in Utah and Montana; she should arrive in Billings by midnight Friday. She'd packed in haste and brought only what she could carry in her oversized duffle.

The rest she carried in a book bag and a small purse that she wore across the front of her body. The remainder of her last two paychecks she had stashed in her boot. She glanced at the couple beside her, newlyweds, she guessed from the lip-lock and their Vegas standard issue matching gold bands. Her gaze darted to the man across the aisle. He sat quietly watching the couple, holding his briefcase close to his side. His expression was dour, disapproving of their public affection. He caught Liberty's curious look and pulled his attaché' closer to his side. Her choices severely limited, she shifted in her seat to look at the black retro wall clock and double-check the time. The soft whispers between the lovers reminded her of the mistake she'd almost made less than a year ago, just after her mother died.

∞

"I suppose you'll be expecting to move back home now that your mother's gone." She'd ridden, not by choice, but by request, by her father in the funeral homes limousine. Funerals were as much a public appearance for her father as any other he showed up for in Vegas. Nothing was left to chance. Appearances meant everything to her father, they always had. Today he was extending his benevolent hand to her... in his own controlling way. Just as she'd seen him manipulate her mother the last years of her life. Liberty knew his game. She'd observed it all her life and only as she'd gotten older had she come to resent and rebel against it.

"Did your housemaid quit again?" she tossed at him, watching row after row of headstones pass by as they left the burial plot.

"Now see there. That's what I'm talking about. I try to extend the olive branch, Liberty Belle and you slap it out of my hand. The problem with you is that you never learned to appreciate everything I gave you."

She responded with a snorting laugh. "You mean, I didn't bow down and kiss your ass every time you decided to remember you had a family?"

His hand shot up, stopping short of smacking her across the face. She held his hard gaze with one of her own. She saw the hate glittering in his black, soulless eyes. She's found out from her mother, only in the few years prior to her death, that she carried a guilt inside her, that she hadn't been strong enough to leave him. Liberty had heard the sounds from beyond closed doors, the sound of him hitting her mother, her tearful pleas to stop. And she ran, as far from the house as she could. She'd been terrified to speak about it to anyone, fearful of what he might to do to her mother. "You touch me and I swear you'll be in the headlines of every paper in town." She kept her voice calm.

He eyed her a moment, chuckled and then lowered his hand, straightening his Armani tie. "Just like your mother."

"Fortunately, she taught me more than you think, because I don't need you and I don't need your money."

He made a sound like he was cleaning his teeth with his tongue. He looked straight ahead. "You'll feel differently when you see how much tuition to that school of yours. Unfortunately, your mother, God-rest-her-soul, nullified her largely inadequate life insurance policy by virtue of how she chose to depart this world."

She leaned forward and tapped on the smoke-glass window shielding them from the driver. The window rolled down. "Pull over here and stop."

He looked over his shoulder, his expression hidden behind his mirrored sunglasses. She caught though the quirk at the corner of his mouth. He probably thought she was certifiable, which was entirely possible. What made her think that she'd see any sorrow, any loss from this sorry excuse she called her father. "I said pull the goddam car over."

"Liberty, you can't just stop the procession. There are well over a hundred cars following us."

She wrenched open the door and the car jerked to a stop. She stepped out and looked back at the long line of vehicles, predominately business people who bottom fed from her father's Vegas club enterprises. "I have all I need from you. You may have given me life, but you've never been a father."

He scooted across the seat; his dark, hateful gaze penetrated her heart. "You get back in the car, this instant you ungrateful—"

Liberty didn't wait for the rest. She slammed the door in his face. A small victory in the memory of her mother against the man who'd pushed her into an early grave. The window rolled down part way as the car lurched forward. "You'll regret this Liberty. You could have had anything you wanted."

"At what price?" she called out to the car as it rolled away. She didn't care if anyone heard her. They all knew how he really was. Most of them lived in fear of his power. Overhead the ominous rain clouds broke free with a single clap of thunder. She turned her face to the skies, letting the rain wash over her face. Pain, fear and an unfathomable loss, pierced her to the core. Tear afresh were lost in the torrents. She opened her arms wide and spoke to the sky. "We're free, momma. We're finally free." A few weeks later, she'd enrolled at the University, taking full responsibility for her loans

It didn't take her long to realize that the part-time waitress position wasn't going to be enough to make ends meet. And like an answer to her silent prayers, she met the devil in the form of exotic Angelo Patreous. He and his friends often stopped in late at night after some of the clubs on the strip had closed. He was a proverbial god, tall, dark and charming, compared to the bleary-eyed drunks that frequented the diner. He was a man of wealth; anyone could see by his designer suits. She discovered that he owned several new clubs in the area and much to Liberty's delight, had no connections with her father—at least, not yet.

"You are a very lovely woman." He'd told her showing off his white even smile. She accepted his flirtatious praise and his generous tips for the expert way she'd serve his pancakes. One thing led to another and she found herself invited to one of his clubs, where he introduced her to his dancers. A few weeks later, she found herself headlining and earning enough to pay off what loans she'd accumulated, rent a nice apartment and convince herself that college was a waste of time as long as she could dance.

"Do you have change for a dollar?"

The fresh-faced new bride pulled Liberty from her reverie. "Oh, sorry. No. Maybe the attendant can help you?"

"Sure, thanks." Her lover could barely let go of her as she struggled to stand.

Liberty readjusted her things, aware that the movement from the young woman had once more stirred the putrid air filtered in from unclean bathrooms. The arrogant looking dark haired lady behind her shifted, sending a sickening waft of heavy perfume around her. She spied a streetlight outside the murky windowpane and considered stepping outside to wait, then realized that she was safer inside, rather than taking her chances with the transients waiting to board without a ticket.

She watched the giggling young woman return to her amorous husband, who wasted no time slipping into the men's bathroom, only to return a few moments later with a handful of bright green condom packets. She looked away.

Their reckless behavior reminded her too much of how she and Angelo once were, before she discovered his expensive cocaine habit and how he skimmed off the girls paychecks to feed his habit. He wasn't going to be happy when he found out that she'd snuck into his office and taken back the twenty percent cut that was rightfully hers. If she could get to this remote ranch, she'd have enough time to figure out what to do next. She drew her jacket closer together and folded her arms over her chest as she looked around her. A low rumble echoed in the deserted streets and she held her breath until the bus turned the corner. She released a sigh with the sound of its air brakes as it pulled into the garage. The sooner she put some distance between her and this town, the better off she'd be.

"May I get this for you?" The dark-eyed man stood when she did.

Liberty grabbed her duffle and swung it over her shoulder with the practiced ease of a combat soldier. Strength and agility were the rewards of her profession. "Thank you, no. I've got it." She walked head high to the bus, and tossed it into the luggage compartment without the driver's assistance.

"One bag, ma'am?" he queried and held out his hand for her ticket and I.D. She produced the information and waited as he eyed her and then the license. "That was taken six years ago."

"Don't forget to renew before your birthday." He smiled and handed it back to her. "Welcome aboard. Your first transfer will be in Salt Lake at our six-fifty a.m. stop."

She nodded her thanks, climbed onto the bus, and searched for an empty set of seats. She found one toward the back of the bus, away from the congested seats up front and placed her bag on the seat beside her to dissuade another from taking a seat. The dark-eyed man caught her eye, and she was grateful when he took a seat next to the perfume-laden woman. The amorous couple, on the other hand, giggled and pawed at each other all the way to the back of the bus.

It was sure to be an interesting next few hours.

She pulled out her iPod, put in her earplugs, and scanned through her music until she found Hearts Greatest Hits to relax her.

What seemed hours later, she was startled awake by an odd sound. Her earpiece had fallen out of her ear, and her skin was cool where she'd been sleeping with her forehead pressed against the window. For a moment, she sat in disoriented fear, until her brain caught up to the fact that she was running away. Liberty glanced at her watch and saw it was almost two in the morning. She craned her neck toward the front and saw most everyone was asleep. Which left the odd sounds coming from behind associated to the newlyweds, unable to wait; it appeared until they reached the hotel.

"Aw, honey, that's it," a male voice cooed. There was a feminine hiss, followed by a soft groan.

She didn't need to look back to know anymore. Liberty shook her head at their audacity. Then again, maybe she was jealous. At least they had each other to share taking such a bold risk. Still, with any luck, they'd be getting off at the first stop. A quiet male groan caused her to chuckle.

Or maybe sooner.

She popped the earplug in to stifle the sounds of their lovemaking and checked her phone for text messages. There were two missed calls both from Elaina, a friend of hers from work. She quickly punched in a text in return. "Are you home and is everything okay? Has Angelo said anything to you?"

A few moments passed before she received a text in response. "He did, but since you refused to say where you were going, it wasn't long before he gave up. Be careful, Libby. If cell phones can be traced, he'll know who to pay to make it happen."

A few hours later when they pulled into Salt Lake, Liberty had deleted all numbers, messages and calls received and dropped her phone in an empty coffee cup and replaced the plastic lid before discarding it in the trash outside the restaurant. She climbed on her transfer bus, glad that the couple as well as the dark-eyed man who gave her the creeps stayed on the other bus, bound for points further east. She was grateful for the room in the near empty bus. She leaned her head against the window and watched the limitless blue sky give way to a dusty twilight, and finally a black velvet sky sprinkled liberally with stars. There were few times she could count that she'd seen the sky awash with stars, the garish lights of Vegas had always blocked them from view. Her eyes drifted shut and the gentle rocking motion of the bus lulled her to sleep.

Dear Readers,

I hope you enjoyed this holiday tale featuring Rein and Liberty's desire and struggle to start a family. I've always loved Liberty's tenacity and courage to not give up. And a revisit to the town of End of the Line always makes me smile and reminds me why I love going back to visit the warm-hearted people of the little Montana town.

If you'd like to read how it all began with one man, Jed Kinnison and the three sons—not of his own blood—that he raised to become his legacy, I invite you to start with: the Kinnison Legacy trilogy:

RUGGED HEARTS
(Wyatt and Aimee)

"Raw Charm...one to read." ~*Publisher's Weekly*

Rugged, quiet, hardworking, Wyatt takes being oldest of the Kinnison family seriously. Scarred early on by the women he'd once trusted his heart to, His sole responsibility now is the welfare of his brothers and the ranch entrusted to them by his stepdad. Forget about things as foolish as love. But that was before he met Aimee and realized a man should never say never to a determined second grade teacher.

Losing her twin sister in a tragic car accident prompts vivacious, resilient Aimee Worth to live out her sister's dream of teaching in a tiny community in End of the Line, Montana. But she never suspected she'd find her Mr. Right. He just doesn't know it yet. Determined, her spirit shatters perceptions that have kept him isolated from life, proving that when it comes to love, the greatest risk is not taking one.

RUSTLER'S HEART, BOOK II
(Rein and Liberty)

Haunted by a tragic past Rein pours himself into creating his Uncle's altruistic goal of making the Last Hope Ranch a haven for the hurt and lost. But a beautiful stranger in the form of a half-sister to the men he calls his brothers arrives and turns his world upside down, bringing with her unseen dangers, not only to his heart, but to the ranch and his family!

Liberty's presence is a surprise to the family she's never met and while she yearns to belong, she knows her presence is a reminder of their painful past. Fearless, she dives in, losing her heart to the ranch, to the community and to an unexpected summer fling that turns to love, only to find that her dangerous past is about to catch up to her and threaten everyone and everything she has come to love.

RENEGADE HEARTS, BOOK III
(Dalton and Angelique)

Dalton has the reputation as a good-timin'man. But this past year his life was upended. With both brothers now married, its' enough to make this bachelor turn on his heel and run. Until the past waltzes back into town, looking more beautiful and less interested than when last they met. Dalton, usually on the run from relationships, finds himself trying to convince Angelique that he's a keeper. And while her kisses imply her attraction, she's holding something back and Dalton's determined to find out her secret.

Angelique's past is the topic of an afternoon talk show—caring for an alcoholic mother, involved in an abusive relationship that nearly cost her and her daughters lives. Fate offer her a second chance to turn things around, but when she returns to End of the Line, sparks fly between her and Dalton and threaten to reveal secrets that could change their lives forever.

And the stories don't stop there! Return to End of the Line, Montana with its heart-warming, well-meaning folks, those hunky country boys and the tenacious women who love them in the spin-off series; Last Hope Ranch:

NO STRINGS ATTACHED
(Clay and Sally)

WELCOME BACK TO END OF THE LINE, MONTANA! Come by for a visit, we think you'll like it here!

Sally Andersen has spent her life teaching school kids and being a caretaker for her ailing father. Alone after five years, she sees her friends marry and start families and decides she, too, wants a family... just not in the conventional way

Serving overseas left Clay Saunders with no leg, PTSD, survivor guilt, and more pity than he wants. Recuperating at the Last Hope ranch at the insistence of his old friends, the Kinnison brothers, he is asked to take part in a charity bachelor auction by the little town's fiery, redheaded music teacher. What Clay doesn't expect is the hope of a normal life that sparks inside of him at her unusual request...

She wants a baby. NO RULES. NO COMMITMENT. NO STRINGS ATTACHED.

There's much more to come from End of the Line! Watch for WORTH THE WAIT and MY ONLY ONE coming in 2017!

About the Author

Amanda McIntyre's storytelling is a natural offshoot of her artistic creativity. A visual writer, living in the rich tapestry of the American heartland, her passion is telling character-driven stories with a penchant (okay, some call it a wicked obsession) for placing ordinary people in extraordinary situations to see how they overcome the obstacles to their HEA

A bestselling author, her work is published internationally in Print, eBook, and Audio. She writes steamy contemporary and sizzling historical romance and truly believes, no matter what, love will always find a way.

Catch all the latest

from Amanda at:

WEBSITE: www.amandamcintyrebooks.com
AMAZON.USA AUTHOR: amazon.com/author/aman-
damcintyre
AMAZON .uk AUTHOR PAGE: www.amazon.
co.uk/-/e/B002C1KH2Q
NEWSLETTER: http://madmimi.com/signups/110714/
join
AUTHORGRAPH: www.authorgraph.com/authors/
AmandaMcIntyre1

Published Books:

Contemporary Romance:

My Only One (A Moonshine novella/Last Hope Ranch crossover)–April 2017

All I Want for Christmas (Kinnison Legacy novella–September. 2016)

Going Home (Sapphire Falls-Kindle World novella–October 2016)

Thunderstruck (Hell Yeah! Kindle World novella–November 2016)

The Way You Look Tonight (RT Vegas anthology, Vol. 3)

No Strings Attached, Book I (Last Hope Ranch)

Rugged Hearts, Book I (Kinnison Legacy)

Rustler's Heart, Book II (Kinnison Legacy

Renegade Hearts, Book III (Kinnison Legacy)

Stranger in Paradise

Tides of Autumn

Unfinished Dreams

Wish You Were Here

Private Party

Mirror, Mirror

Historical/Erotic Romance:

A Warrior's Heart (western historical) (October 2016)

The Promise (December 2016**)**

The Dark Seduction of Miss Jane (erotic thriller)

The Master & the Muses ★

The Diary of Cozette ★

Tortured ★
The Pleasure Garden ★
Winter's Desire ★
Dark Pleasures ★
Para/Fantasy:
Tirnan 'Oge
★Starred are available also in audio and internationally

62665907R00083

Made in the USA
Charleston, SC
20 October 2016